THEO WANTS

MMF / MM ROMANCE

JESS SAVAGE

1
———

THEO

I'm so nervous I jerk off twice in the shower so I don't explode before I even get touched by Oneida.

Like everything else in the world, the shower stall isn't made for me and I have to duck to get my head under the water and wash my hair after.

They say being tall is an advantage. I've seen the tinder takedowns on Twitter where broads demand, "6 foot or don't bother." But practically speaking? Being tall is a huge pain in the ass.

For one thing, I always wear shorts because it's hard to find pants that don't hang above my ankles.

Where's the flood, Theo?

HA frigging HA.

How's the weather up there?

Wasn't funny the first five hundred times. Cars, countertops, *everything* except basketball hoops are made for the average person, not me. But the worst is that while most girls *do* seem to love me being tall, I never feel comfortable having to stoop down to talk to them. They seem tiny and fragile. One wrong move and I'd break them. And I make plenty of wrong moves.

Oneida's tall at least, so I'm feeling good about that. She's also old, but the kind that whispers she knows what to do with a guy, that she'll take control. That's definitely what I'm paying for.

Oneida is also an all-caps LEGEND around the club, the most high-class lay you can have in this town. All a man had to do was say her name in the locker room at Rolling Green and every dude in there would break into schoolboy giggles.

I'd asked what they meant a couple times.

"This joker!" They'd point and laugh at me.

Later, Dad made me solemnly swear to never mention her name— not to my friends, not to my enemies, and especially not to my mom. Knowing about Oneida was one of the perks of belonging to the club, not information for just anyone.

Fast forward to present day: me, about to go off to college, still a freaking virgin. *Whatthefrick,* right? I lettered in varsity basketball, I'm an A student, my dad sits on the board at Sierra Vista Hospital, and my best friend is literally spending the summer in a threesome. I don't know what I was doing wrong.

OK, maybe I do know.

The truth is, girls seem like people when we're hanging out, working on a project together. But once I cross that line into trying to get them naked, I start acting like a robot, saying stupid, nervous stuff. Things that are sexy in porn— tits and naked bodies and grunting, writhing movements— they just don't translate to the girls I know in real life.

Take Hailey for example. I've been trying to date her all summer. Like, seriously making an effort— taking her out to the movies, showing up at her work. If I could've just fast-forwarded to the part where she was naked, I'm pretty sure I could've done it.

But all those steps in between? I sucked.

Turned out she was balling Jack the whole summer anyway, a third of his threesome. The one piece of luck I got this summer was catching all of them in the act and having the good sense to pull out my phone and document.

Which is how I paid for a night with Oneida.

Or more accurately, how I convinced Jack and his two girlfriends to pay for Oneida.

Blackmail's an ugly word, but you have to see my side of things. First off, they had the money. Second, I was doing them a favor by keeping quiet. And third?

The third part is steadily filling me with panic, because right now? I'm the best I'll ever be— living in a town where everyone knows I'm a sports god, from a good family, smart to boot. In a few weeks, I'll go off to college and be a squeaky new freshman with no chance of scoring.

That's why I this thing with Oneida is exactly what I need. A lesson, a private tutor to get me acclimated; show me the steps to get from 'hi' to sex.

I tell myself it isn't any different from a golf or tennis lesson— some skill you need to fit into the world, and instead of learning it on your own, you hired a professional to show you the ropes. And of course, you convince your friends to pool resources and get it for you as a gift. When those three cooled off, they'd remember it was me, Theo, and that I would never actually out them. I practically said as much to Ella.

I stare at my reflection in the mirror. I'm cut: six-pack, pecs, guns, quads. That's not opinion, it's just how it is. Which, trust me, makes the fact I can't score even more humiliating. It means I am perpetually cock-blocking myself somehow. It's either my personality or acne. That's a fact too: my face is always blotchy red with some breakouts, my stubble at war with my skin.

Sometimes I hate being me, so I get why other people hate me too.

I give my junk a rubdown and get dressed, spritzing body spray on my chest for courage. I don't dare to go for a third wank before Oneida. That kind of thing could backfire and leave me noodle-dicked.

I get dressed, change my mind, and re-dress. I think about what she'll do to me, if it'll compare to what I saw Hailey, Jack, and Ella doing.

Instead of Jack being my wingman, Lucas shows to pick me up, exactly on time.

Lucas and I went to school together, but we aren't that close. He doesn't like me for some reason, even though we were both jocks at school. He's average height, which makes him shorter than me, and he's built like a bodybuilder or a wrestler— wide shoulders, narrow waist, thick thighs.

He rings the doorbell like my fricking date, and I rush to get it before Mom answers. It's a joke that I'm even worried about it.

"Who is it?" she calls from the living room, sounding like she's well into her second glass of wine.

"A friend. From Rolling Green," I add to keep her from being curious. She hates that Dad spends so much time at that place. I open the door, and—

"Hey." The wind is absolutely knocked out of me.

Lucas works at Rolling Green, a pool boy, slinging drinks from the cabana for all the summer brats and sad house-wives. My mom would be one of them if she didn't loathe the place.

I'm used to Lucas in his pool boy garb, his sardonic

smile, his professionally off-limits attitude. Or even back in school— casual T-shirts and jeans that bagged at his ankles. Sometimes a thin gold chain at his neck. When I'd get bored in pre-Calc, I'd stare at how it peeked out from his shirt, winding across the back of his neck. His thick, charcoal hair would get longer and longer over the weeks until the chain disappeared. Then the freshly shorn neck stubble and visible chain again.

I aced pre-Calc. In case you're thinking I was distracted. I wasn't. I just notice things.

Lucas stands on my step in a tight white T-shirt and dark jeans, looking like I've only seen him a few times— like he's ready to go out and have a good time. He's just my ride to Oneida's. Oneida's pimp somehow, even though he's my age and she's like... way older.

I pull the door closed behind me. That means stepping out, closer to him. He doesn't step back. I can smell his after-shave. Frick, my pulse hammers so hard I'm sure he sees.

It's finally time to lose my godforsaken virginity.

2

THEO

"You ready?" Lucas asks.

"Let's go."

There's a moment he doesn't move, and we are too close together. He smiles, all cocky and smug. Probably testing to see if I'm gonna back out.

"Come on," I say to get him moving. The clock is ticking, and I don't want to be late.

Lucas has me right where he wants me— just some plebe desperate to do the one thing every other guy in the world accomplishes without paying for it. Whatever. I'm so fricking ready to get this done that I don't even care about embarrassment.

I am literally *minutes* from getting laid.

He turns and walks down the steps to the car, gets in the driver's seat.

Is this a chauffeur situation? Do I sit in the front or the back?

I get in back, knees practically jammed into the back of the front seat. The look Lucas gives me lets me know I'm being a dipshit somehow.

"Hold on." I get out, get in front, where now I'm in danger of kneeing myself in the face at a sharp stop.

Sitting next to him, I push the seat back, sighing contentedly at the increased livable space. Doesn't help that my head brushes the ceiling of his crap car.

Lucas takes all this in with an expression that makes me feel like I'm an exhibit at the circus.

"What?" I demanded.

"Nothing." He puts the car in drive. "I just didn't realize how tall you are."

"What is this, a car for ants?" I grunt, and Lucas makes a noise that might be a laugh.

* * *

We drive in silence, intimately close together in the small car. It's fricking confusing since my dick only wants to think about what's imminent.

I drum my fingers on my thigh. Am I the first guy from our class Lucas has taken to Oneida's? That seems like one of those questions that makes people not like me, so I don't ask, even though I'm curious.

"So how long does this take?" I ask him instead.

He cuts his eyes over, one hand on the steering wheel like he thinks he's in a hot guy ad. The twilight sky makes his dark eyes liquid with amusement. "That's up to you, bro."

This guy is going to know down to the minute how long it takes me to nut. Despite this humiliation, my sausage plumps. Doesn't help that his aftershave smells freaking awesome. I almost ask him what it is, but catch myself at the last minute. Guys don't ask other guys questions like that.

"Ever get repeat customers?" I ask.

He nods, eyes on the road now. "Sure."

"And is it just straight sex or can do get like... special requests?" I think of the video that got me here— my best friend Jack with his hand inside my would-be girlfriend Hailey's shorts while his long-time girlfriend Ella jerked him off. I swallow nervously.

Those liquid eyes slide back to me, amused, confident, completely at ease.

"Screw you man," I sulk. "I'm just trying to pass the time."

"What do you want, a menu?"

"Honestly? Yeah. If you're gonna do an enterprise like this, why does it have to be all cloak and dagger? How do I know I'm gonna get what I want?"

"What *do* you want?"

"Come on. What I *don't* want is to go in there, get a dry rub hand job, and get told that's where my fifteen hundred went, and if I want to put it in wet, I gotta fork over another grand."

"First off," Lucas says. "There's not a thousand dollar difference between a hand job and a wet fuck."

My dick goes rock hard. Like, difficult to breathe hard. Up until this moment, he was still Lucas from my classes all through high school, a teammate for some sports, the Dodge Ball King in middle school. In all that time, I've joked plenty about sex with the guys. But not him. He was always above it all.

"I could get laid for free, you know," I finally manage, slumping down in the seat to adjust my shorts.

Lucas makes a noncommittal noise, like *maybe yes, maybe no*. I hate that he knew me in school and can make his own judgment on my skills. "So what is it you're looking for?"

"What do you mean?" I demand, angry at feeling exposed.

"Usually guys who ask are looking for something specific."

It gives me a chill he knows what guys ask for. Lots of guys. And what I want is roaring up from my toes. *Maybe I want to try you instead.*

What the freaking fuck? What the freaking fuck was that thought?!

I am here on a mission: Lose my virginity to some broad who knows everything and will do it all. I just have to lay back and have it done. Like a tattoo. Like a massage. That's what I want. It's Jack's stupid video that messed me up, and my own overloaded ball sack that will absolutely not give me a moment's peace with every kinky thing it can imagine.

"Ever do threesomes?" I hear myself saying. Frick. I should've had a drink before I got in the car. Then at least I'd have an excuse for talking like this.

"Sure," Lucas says. "What kind?"

I reach for his dash and flick the vents hard. They snap at each movement, back and forth. Any self-respecting guy would assume a threesome involves a pussy sandwich, one meat in the middle. There must be something that gives me away. Maybe that was what the girls who turned me down saw.

I laugh under my breath and look out the window. I want to be rude as hell to him for insulting me with that question. But I don't. There's something about him. He's so nonjudgmental when he says it. It keeps my anger in check.

The night sky is violet strewn with inky clouds, the temperature dropping outside. I shiver, even though it's only cold in comparison to the heat of the day. We are almost there. The car slows, creeping through a neighborhood.

This is the night I become a real man.

All the other club members who have been inside Oneida, we are like frat brothers, members of a not-so-secret club.

"How long have you been doing this?" I ask.

"What do you mean?"

"Pimpin', bro." I elbow him across the seats. "How'd you get this sweet business internship with the elite of Rolling Green?"

"Fuck you, man," he deflects my question, laughing.

"You on the menu?" I joke back. "How much would it cost me?"

I tell myself I'm asking because I want him to tell me to fuck off for real, to be pissed. I want to re-establish the fact that I'm the paying customer, that I can buy and sell Lucas' ass, and he'd better remember it.

Especially if we ever see each other at a party when I come home from school. I need the upper hand with him.

But he doesn't get defensive. The less bothered he seems, the harder it is for me to breathe. It's just the two of us in the close space of the car, and I have this insane impulse to lean across and...

What? Man, I don't even know. Like every other attempt to get in someone's pants, I'm clueless about how these things work. All I know is I'm probably messing it up with my stupid mouth.

"Maybe," Lucas says. "You into that kind of thing?"

This whole conversation is making me feel even more like he is the one in control. "How much do you get to take it in the ass?"

In my head, it sounds like an insult, a taunting joke that should make him squirm with humiliation. But I hear how it comes out. Like we are negotiating.

Frick. How am I in this situation? It's his cologne. Every time Lucas moves, I catch a whiff of it, like my nose is against his skin. But I don't crack the window. I'm pissed... but I don't want this to stop either. Not until I figure out how to establish that I am the boss with him. Otherwise...

Already, I can see him at the next kegger, surrounded by my friends, telling the story of me losing my virginity, people laughing until they fall over.

Lucas' knuckles are easy on the steering wheel, his fore-arms flexing as he turns the wheel. He looks like he could power jack a guy off for days without getting tired. "I can go in with you when we get to Oneida's."

"What's that cost?" I use careful control to open the vent in the dash, pushing my fingers along the grates.

If he has a price, and I know it, he'll never dare make fun of me at some drunken party. That's how things like this work— he has something on me, I have something on him — we stay friends through fear of mutual destruction.

"Depends," he says, "We can figure it out as we go."

I swallow. The lump in my throat is not nearly the hardest thing about me.

It would be good to have a wingman. All the times I've gone to a strip club have been with a group of hard-ons like me, laughing and gawking. I've even watched porn with some of the basketball team. Hell, even when I watch porn by myself, there's a guy on the video.

The car pulls into the drive of a modest cottage with a manicured topiary lawn. The front windows are dark, but I can see a porch light on in the back.

"Yeah. Yeah, OK," I agree, hoarse, and unclick my seatbelt.

Having him there means I won't have to break the ice with Oneida by myself, like all the other dates I've been on where I can't think of a thing to say. I flex my thighs like 20 times to get my dick to ease up enough that I don't flagship when I get out of the car.

I think again about the video of Jack, Hailey, and Ella. *Everyone's doing it like this,* I tell myself. *Totally not weird that Lucas is going with you.*

The engine cuts and I pry myself out of his tiny car, losing its cradling warmth. I miss it immediately, and when Lucas meets me on the drive, I try to stand a little closer in a nonobvious way. Just for moral support. Now that we are here, I am scared. Not nervous, or full of braying laughter, but actually really scared. What we're doing is illegal.

"Come on," Lucas says.

I let go of the idea of being in control.

Whatever happens tonight is because I paid for it. Like a massage, or a tattoo. I am going to let them do things to me.

Which is about when I decide I didn't care what it costs, I have to have whatever I want tonight. I deserve it.

And no one else has to know.

3

———

Lucas

I wait in my car in front of the Benedict place a solid three minutes before I get out to get Theo. Blue television light flickers across the curtains in what I assume must be his living room, soft warm glow of lamplight in the upstairs windows. It's a McMansion— sprawling square footage on a small lot for a small carbon footprint, new landscaping, neighbors close on purpose.

Theo's dad sits on the board at Sierra Vista Medical Center. It's a for-profit hospital that only takes my sister's insurance a quarter of the time. The house Theo lives in was paid for by working-class people like my mom, and the out-of-pocket cash they put into the system.

According to google maps, they have a pool in the back. Costs $30,000-$60,000 to install a pool around here, one like the kind they have. Thirty thousand dollars would go a long way toward extending Kit's quality of life. Hell, even an actual pool, where she could float weightlessly above the pain and swelling of her aching body, would go a long way.

I tell myself to stop feeling sorry for myself, get my head in the game.

I wonder if Theo's dad knows what's happening tonight, the fucked up circle of life that is me screwing money out of Theo while Theo's dad screws money out of my family. The thought makes me smirk bitterly. I lope up the front walk and ring the bell.

The door whooshes open. Theo's tall, athletic build blocks most of my view of the home's interior, although I hear some reality show going in the background. Theo pulls the door closed behind him, nearly bumping into me in his hurry to get going.

Theo and I have known each other a long time, but we've never been more than passing acquaintances. He's a good-looking guy, popular, athletic, good student. He also has a tendency to put his foot in his mouth any chance he gets, and he's hurt the feelings of more than one of my friends with a thoughtless comment or ten. But hey, that's high school. I'll admit it to anyone that we're all assholes in high school. And high school's over.

Things I currently know about Theo:

He's blackmailing Hailey.

Hailey's dating Jack.

Theo and Jack are best friends.

Jack paid me for video of Theo getting serviced by Oneida, my boss.

So tonight, the lucky guy in front of me is about to star in a very small circulation level porn, which will probably be used as some sort of revenge and/or blackmail.

For a fleeting moment, I feel a slight twinge of guilt.

Theo's exactly like I remember him. Gets in the car, gets out. Knees up to his ears until he pushes the seat as far back as it will go, and complains like it's the car's fault. If he keeps this up, Oneida's gonna get her riding crop out and teach him some manners. Should I warn him?

"What is this, a car for ants?" Theo grunts and I decide this will be way more fun if I don't.

* * *

I've been doing this for maybe six months now, and on every date, I learn something new. People I never would've guessed have ridden in my car, pretending they don't know me. In fact, Theo's the first to both know me *and* strike up a conversation. I wonder what he's doing here. He's an attractive guy... if you like the arrogant asshole type. Lots of girls sure seem to. The guy should have zero problems getting laid for free.

Theo drums his fingers. "So how long does this take?"

Oh, OK, except his personality. He can be abrasive. That doesn't really bother me. You always know what Theo's thinking. Like now. I laugh. "That's up to you, bro."

When I manage a glance over at him and our eyes meet, there is this weird... crackle of energy. It takes me by surprise.

His body fills the car, long legs jittering with nervous energy. Probably he's excited to spend time with Oneida, and I'm just catching a whiff of his pheromones. His arm hangs over our shared armrest, and every once in a while, his arm hairs brush me. The sensation sends shivers up my spine.

"You ever get repeat customers?" he asks. This might be the first real conversation I've ever had with Theo that didn't involve being in the same assigned group for a class project. "And is it just straight sex or can you get like... special requests?"

I shift in my seat. Is this why he's here? The usual high school prom queen won't satisfy?

"Screw you man," he mutters. "I'm just trying to pass the time."

Ah, and here's the Theo I'm acquainted with, acting like some brat at Rolling Green, like he's gonna send back the chef's special because he wants what he wants when he wants it.

"What *do* you want?" I ask because I can't resist taunting him a little.

I know I shouldn't, but I kind of like him like this, slowly losing control. At least in this car, I know everything. Except for what he's looking to get from Oneida. And to do my job, I need to have that key piece of data, to let her know how to please her customer.

If Theo chickens out, O and I will of course still keep the fifteen hundred fee for her time. But the much bigger amount I charged to get video will probably have to go back. That money's as good as spent. I need to make this go smoothly.

Theo says, "Come on. What I *don't* want is to go in there, get a dry rub hand job, and get told that's where the fifteen hundred went, and if I want to put it in wet, I gotta fork over another grand."

OK, he needs to calm that shit down. Oneida will not want to be whined at.

"First off," I say. "There's not a thousand dollar difference between a hand job and a wet fuck."

Our eyes lock again, and there's another extremely weird zing of chemistry. Have I harbored a longstanding thing for Theo effing Benedict all these years? For a moment, I can't tear my eyes away from him.

"I could get laid for free, you know," he says.

Does he hear himself right now? It makes me want to laugh out loud.

When I do, I realize how long it's been. I've spent most of the last three years worrying about Kit and bills. It's been a blur of going to the doctor's office, scheduling an appointment to see some specialist, sitting on hold with her insurance, or cooking dinner while I wait for Mom and Kit to come home.

Honestly, when I spent the last two years of high school harboring some major crushes on a few of her doctors, it made sense— they were saving her life. Who didn't want to nail a superhero in scrubs?

I didn't really have time to debate with myself about the fact most of her doctors were guys— there was too much other bullshit going on. And anyway, it was all for nothing— my fantasies of meeting one of them in a Grey's Anatomy style locker room and starting something never went further than my imagination. I wasn't even sure I was gay— I just had limited options and a lot of needy frustration. Any fantasy to get away from reality.

"So... what is it you're looking for?" I ask. Time to seal this deal and drop him at O's.

"What do you mean?" Theo sounds nervous.

When his eyes drop, they fall to my quads as I let up on the gas and move to the brake. "Usually guys who ask are looking for something specific."

"Ever do threesomes?"

Is he asking me to join or just bullshitting? I've never worked with Oneida. We're like Navy Seals that way — each of us an expert in our own field.

"How long have you been doing this?" Theo asks in a quiet voice, and my pulse thuds.

"What do you mean?" But I know. He's asking if I'm available. It flashes through my mind: touching him, kissing him...

"Pimpin', bro." Theo laughs, and I'm instantly let down. He's toying with me.

"Fuck you, man," I laugh despite myself. He's so fucking likable, even when he's being an ass. Maybe *because* he's an ass, I don't have to take him seriously.

Theo taps his thigh with a balled fist, and everything becomes clear: He's never been with a woman. He's not asking about Oneida, he's asking about me. The zing between us is so subtle maybe Theo doesn't even know what it is. But I do.

For a long time, he stares out the window. The heat of his body radiates, making me warm wherever we nearly touch. This whole night has taken me by surprise, shaken me out of my bored worry, all my thoughts about keeping my house together. Theo and his ridiculous bravado and perfect jawline are like a vacation from the life I've been living.

He brushes knuckles against the door handle like he imagines flinging it open and escaping. "How much do you get to take it in the ass?"

My head hears it and thinks it's an insult, but my cock hears it and knows it's an offer.

He looks like a guy at war with himself, his face strained. That raises a yellow flag. For Theo and honestly for Oneida too. She keeps most guys on a short leash with her caustic attitude, but physically, she's a lightweight. She doesn't need a guy in there with her who might get spooked or even aggressive. My job is to make sure she's safe.

I say, "I can go in with you when you go into Oneida's."

He opens his mouth, breathing in slow inhales and panting exhales— something I've seen him do on the basketball court, like he's been trained to do that to keep his wits about him, to calm down his adrenaline.

For all his bravado, I think he's scared. Men are supposed to be only excited about sex, talk about it like it's a game where you score. But it's a very human thing, messy and nerve-wracking and funny and sometimes sad. When I get around to writing real college application essays, I'll wish I could talk all about the humanity I've seen being an escort.

I say, "We can figure it out as we go."

And for once, Theo doesn't have a smartass comeback.

I pull into the cottage's driveway and park. I can almost feel Theo trembling in his seat, and it makes my heart tender and my dick weirdly hard. I worked this job long enough to feel confident in almost everything I do here.

I wait until he looks over at me, ready. The thing I'm getting about Theo is he likes to be in control. Oneida's gonna have fun torturing him about that, but for me, I don't mind letting him be the boss. He swallows, nods.

"Come on," I say.

$$4$$

____

LUCAS

The cottage smells like fresh baked cookies, which is technically accurate— Oneida buys premade dough and puts it in the oven an hour before her dates with new customers. The smell relaxes people, and a plate of cookies is welcoming, something a client can do with their hands if they aren't ready to fall into bed right away. It feels a little like a mom thing to me, but I'm not the kind of guy who'd go to Oneida, and she knows clientele well enough to be a rich woman off them.

"The truth is, most of them want to talk," she'd told me early on. "Sometimes I'll give them a cookie or a glass of wine, set them on the couch, and..." She shrugs.

The house is set up like a vacation rental: a living room with a nice couch and a fireplace is where all new clients start. If you take them into the bedroom right away, some spook.

Theo takes in the cozy living room as Oneida comes from the kitchen. She is a winner of the genetic lottery, beautiful and intimidating, and she swoops in, excitedly calling Theo's name. She hands him a drink.

"I think I owe you this," she winks and hands him a glass of dark liquid.

Theo grins and takes it from her.

"So what are you boys up to tonight?" she teases as he knocks the drink back. He immediately coughs, sputtering.

In a different situation, I might laugh— after all, it's Theo. But my job in this room is to stay quiet and let the john get comfortable. Clients who get embarrassed or too nervous can get mean and unpredictable. They can bolt and then want a refund, they can get unruly. Oneida will give me a cue to let me know when she feels good about me making a quiet exit so they can get to business.

So I don't laugh. I thump Theo on the back, leaning into him so our sides touch. I don't say anything. Theo does better when he doesn't have to talk.

"Would you like to sit in the living room for a bit, or go back to the bedroom?" Oneida asks.

Theo coughs again. His eyes dart to mine.

"Hey O, can I stay awhile? Just until you two get settled?" I ask, so Theo doesn't have to. He nods slightly.

"Of course," Oneida answers smoothly. "Would you two like the room?" she adds. Probably Theo's not the first dude who showed up for a straight fuck and turned out to want something entirely different?

Theo shakes his head. I can tell Oneida's not entirely sure what to make of this. She is graceful and seductive, touching Theo's forearm as she gestures toward the couch. The really sexy thing about Oneida is how she uses her eyes. She watches you like you are the most important man on earth. She notices every change in your expression. Sometimes it's almost as though she can read your mind.

"Of course. We can do whatever you like," she simpers. "Why don't we start off with the formalities."

She waves a hand to let us all know how gauche it is to talk of money. When Theo doesn't take the hint, she prompts, "Let me get a card from you."

"I thought... I thought everything was already paid?" Theo is definitely right where Oneida wants him— horny and unsure and willing to do anything to get into that back bedroom.

She leans in, and the top of her dress gives him a view of her beautifully carved collarbones, the slope of her breast. "To cover anything we might do beyond what we're scheduled for."

"Is there a menu or something?" Theo mumbles.

She laughs, touching his chest lightly. "Aren't you fun?"

She passes by the lit fireplace as she goes to the kitchen, letting Theo admire all her curves, the gauzy kaftan she's wearing illuminated by firelight to show how little she has on underneath.

As she gets her billing square, Theo leans into me for support. His excitement gets me going. It's just a hazard of the job— when a client gets ready to fuck, I'm transformed from Regular Lucas into Gigolo Lucas, and it doesn't embarrass me to get hard or to notice Theo noticing. If I let myself get embarrassed, I'll have to find another job, and I can't do that. Not if I want to get out of the debt my family's in. Or enjoy my work. And I *do* enjoy the work.

Oneida returns with her phone and the little white square attached.

Theo puts his hand into his back pocket. "What is this going to show up as on my bill, if I do... you know, extra stuff?"

"I'm a life coach," Oneida says matter of factly. There is, in fact, a framed Life Coach certificate in the hallway leading to the bedroom. "You're here for a session, and whatever you say or do in a session is completely confidential."

"How much? For..." He swallows.

She raises an eyebrow, a catlike smile crossing her face. She moves a step closer. "Maybe you can't afford us."

Us. Guess Oneida knows her clientele. I am completely rock hard.

"I'm here for you, for the next two hours." Oneida moves so close to him she could kiss his neck... or get up on tiptoe to kiss his face. "... but Lucas' time is valuable too."

"Can't I get a beginner's special or something?"

Oneida laughs, brushing so close and so accurately against him, only her nipples touch. They poke through the thin fabric, her areolas big and rouged.

Theo wears shorts as a rule, and I can see him tenting out when she steps back. It sends a throb of wanting through me. I'm not sure I want to stay. But if I get sent away, I'm gonna have to punch something. I have never been in the room this long with Oneida and her client.

I pull back, letting the two of them start up whatever they're going to do.

Theo grabs my wrist and that zing, that fucking ball=tightening chemistry between us catches me and I inhale sharply. Oneida cuts her eyes at me, slow smile like she knows something I don't want her to. Maybe she just thinks it's funny that I'm going to be on Theo's blackmail tape.

She plucks Theo's credit card from his pinched fingers and gets to work setting up a payment.

Theo's grip tightens and I feel him getting nervous like

he might bolt. The scent of his skin fills my nostrils and I know he's sweating, but the smell just turns me on more. I clear my throat to get Oneida's attention, warn her she's stressing him out.

She looks up, reads the room, and notes Theo holding my wrist. She sets the phone and credit card aside.

"Come sit down," she coaxes Theo further into the room, smiling coyly at him. Her nipples show under the thin material of her kaftan.

Theo goes tense next to me— tall and muscular boy, about to run for the door. If he leaves, we'll lose the video money. But that's not the first thought that goes through my head. The first thing is: *If he leaves, I'll lose my chance with him.*

The real Theo and Lucas would never hook up. He's a rich boy, destined to become a lawyer or a real estate mogul, end up with a lifetime membership to whatever country club is the most exclusive in his town. As soon as he starts pulling in money, he'll get laid like crazy, and then he will be so far out of my league I'll never again enjoy the simple pleasure of watching him cram his giant frame into my car.

Which is almost how it is now, with the difference in our social standings. But tonight, I could have him. And better yet, I could have him in a way that neither of us would ever talk about again. Because eventually, he's gonna know we're taping this, which cuts down on Theo's likelihood of ever trusting me again, much less of wanting to go to bed with me. It will be our dirty little secret.

My dick is so hard, it's difficult to think. Oneida kisses him, and he bends to kiss her back. She takes his hand— the one not still holding my wrist— and tugs him toward the couch. This is my cue to exit.

But Theo throws an anxious look my way. Probably if he'd opened his mouth, he would've immediately stuck his big fat foot in it with some bromophoic comment where I'd feel no choice but to laugh at him or get the fuck out of there.

But he doesn't. Just pleads silently with me, eyes huge. And that big, calloused hand that's holding my wrist? It slides down to take my hand, palm to palm, as he brings me to the couch with him.

Once he makes his decision, things move smoothly as clockwork.

He sits on the couch, center cushion, manspreading like always, cock making his shorts a pup tent. I crash next to him, mimicking his stance, like we're at Oneida's about to watch the big game, our thighs touching.

Oneida stands between his open legs and bends down to kiss him, her loose shift falling away from her body. Theo puts his hand on her waist, then moves up to her tits. He makes this little uncontrollable sigh that reverberates through me. Oneida lets the kaftan drop to the floor with a wiggle of her shoulders.

She has a beautiful body, even at her age. If there was high watt overhead lighting, I'd probably spot some scars from the cosmetic surgery, the tucks and nips and implants. Oneida's body is definitely not that of a twenty-something, just like her attitude isn't girlish. In front of us, she is just as gorgeous as she is exotic. She is tight and hard and strong, the faint tan lines from her bikini, the sparkling chain around her waist, the definition at her abs. She also doesn't seem to mind that I'm right there with front row seats to this. And like everything else about her, that makes Oneida irresistible.

Theo lets go of my hand to touch her, and I keep thinking how any minute, she'll drag him back to the bedroom, or he'll tell me to go. I try to keep as still as possible, like maybe they'll forget I'm here. I may unload in my pants without a single touch.

Usually, my gigolo hookups have been exclusively with women from Rolling Green. They are soft and vulnerable, feisty and demanding, or with a thin crackling of surface ice, but they all want the same thing— someone who doesn't have to be told what to do to make them happy. After the sex, they want to be held. They like little caresses on their shoulder or when I stroke their hair. They want me to listen to their days, or to hold them as they cry and tell me their husbands broke their hearts. Some try to co-opt me— offer to have me live in their guest houses, take their children to school, do some light housework and be available a few times a week for sex.

Can't lie, I've considered it. I tell each of them they could get a proper boyfriend to do these things for free, men who will adore them and worship them as I do. They just look at me like I don't know what assholes men can be.

Oneida wriggles her body down Theo's. She lifts his shirt up over his head and presses her breasts against his bare chest. His legs flex around her.

"You are so beautiful," he says.

He doesn't need me here anymore, he's doing fine. I should figure out a way to get out of the room before they are actually in the act. I'm probably in the video's frame. Oneida will edit it to have as little of me in it as possible, but I might as well make it easier for her.

I'm thinking all this in the rational part of my head. But my dick is definitely not listening. My hips aren't even listening, and they keep flexing under my pants like I want to thrust myself into them. My mouth is open, my exhales jagged.

I ease off the cushion, separating from them. I don't say anything. They are clearly too into each other to notice.

Theo gasps as she hooks her fingers under his waistband and begins to tug. "Lift up," she says.

OK, I've definitely overstayed my welcome.

Theo grabs my forearm again. I freeze. He should be entranced with Oneida. If I were in his shoes, I'd be more worried a guy would see me prematurely ejaculate all over my own shorts, game over. As it is, I'm kind of worried about that for myself anyway.

"Stay?" There's none of his on-brand bravado, just longing.

Oneida goes still. "Is this OK?" she asks him.

She doesn't want anything on film that could come back on us. The chief of police is one of Oneida's clients, but even he couldn't protect us for long if there was something on the tape that made us look as though we'd pushed Theo into something he didn't want.

"Yeah," Theo says. "This is so good."

He doesn't let go of me though.

Oneida pulls down his shorts, and his cock springs free. My mouth parts with intense wanting. He's thick and big, veined and rigid. His private smell warms the air. Almost immediately, Oneida drags her boobs over his exposed member, and Theo groans.

I have never been so hard at the job before. A throb goes through my cock that makes me feel like I'm going to lose control.

"Kiss it," he says, eyes hazy.

She takes him into her mouth, red lipstick marking him.

This is not like watching porn. Everything here is real.

The smell of them, the brush of his thigh against mine as he moves, the sound of his quiet grunts and moans, the faint squeak of couch springs. The rhythm of her head in his lap.

The overwhelming urge to join them stuns me. What am I doing here? These people are literally fucking, it is high time I showed myself the exit.

I am on fire— my bottom lip as I touch my tongue to it, the shift of my pants against my thighs, the cotton containment of my tighty-whities, which are 100% me as I thought my job would end at the door tonight.

The slurping sound Oneida makes nearly sends Theo over the edge. They are really getting into it now as he stretches, tilting his hips as she goes down like he wants to hit the back of her throat. Her dark hair cascades down his thigh, obscuring my view, but the facts keep crashing into my brain: they are doing it. They are doing it right next to me and any minute now, he's going to shoot his load down her throat.

I make the slightest noise, uncontrollable, because it's killing me to sit here and watch.

Theo looks at me, eyes heavy-lidded and mouth slack. He's got thick golden-black lashes, strong, perfect eyebrows, a runner's leanness that carves his jaw. It's been so long since I've wanted anyone real, I feel wild with it.

That's probably a critical error for a gigolo. Especially one who knows this whole thing is being filmed.

Fuck it, I decide on the fly. *I don't care.* I lean into him, an invitation. More than that. A request.

"Kiss me," he orders.

I bend to drop a kiss on his shoulder, the starchy cotton of his T-shirt, dragging it up so I can kiss his chest, his ribcage. I want that. I want to know what he'll feel like in my mouth, taste like.

He stops me and my face burns— the embarrassment of sudden, firm-handed rejection. I'm so turned on I've made a tactical error, heard what I wanted to hear.

"Kiss me," he says again, his hips flexing, rhythmic now, like he's going to shoot his load soon. His upper lip curls away from his teeth. The knowledge makes my cock surge, tingles and chills all across my body.

Theo leans into me, bending down because the guy's a skyscraper. His mouth lands on mine.

I've never kissed a guy before. Not for business or for fun. I've thought about it though, what it'd be like, some stolen moment in the hospital lounge with a hot doctor, some frantic, forbidden thing. Because you're not supposed to fuck your sister's health providers.

This has all of that, all that tainted illegality to it that makes my pulse race. His tongue explores my mouth. When Theo Benedict isn't actively trying to be an asshole, he's fucking hot as hell. He pushes my mouth open wider. This close I can feel Oneida bobbing toward his climax, and I want to slow her down, make it last.

But she knows her business better than I do, and Theo breaks the kiss to catch his breath, holding his forehead head against mine, like I'm some key part. His hips move in that familiar, primal rhythm, teetering at the edge of control.

He touches his lips to mine, his hand wrapping around the base of my neck to bring me close, taking in the buzz-cut hair at the base of my skull. *He's tasting me,* I think, and almost cum, nudging uncontrollably against his thigh, reaching for his hand.

I find it and press his palm against my upper thigh. The feel, foreign, so different than anyone else.

I put my hand over his and guide him to my cock. He groans. Cums. Shudders as Oneida gags on the length of him. Maybe for show, or maybe because he really has a huge cock. She takes it in stride, staying on him until he relaxes, still kissing me. But now gentle, like a thank you, or an apology.

I am so hard I might die.

5

—————

You probably think I'm the villain right now, what with letting Theo fall dick first into a blackmail video. Honestly? It doesn't feel great to me either. But there's a lot of grey area moral and legal stuff you have to do to be successful in this job, and I need this job.

So I do with the knowledge there's video running somewhere in this house the same thing I do with all the other stuff I see and hear while working as a gigolo. I toss that knowledge in a box marked "Work Stuff, Don't Touch" somewhere in the back of my head, and I mind the warning label.

OK, even that's not entirely the whole honest story, but we can talk about the other piece later.

Because what I want to focus on now is how I keep kissing Theo on his way out of Oneida's place. Blushing Theo, laughing Theo. Adorable, awkward, happy Theo, big feet and hands like an overgrown puppy.

I kiss his cheek. I kiss his mouth as Oneida runs his

credit card. Theo doesn't ask how much and I don't care. Not being able to keep my hands off him isn't an angle. I just know what will happen next, and I want that moment where he is happy, where *we* are happy. At Oneida's, you learn to live in the moment.

He presses against me and I groan as I feel the pressure of his thigh against my hard-on. The sound of him laughing against my mouth. The power dynamic shifts in his favor, because we both know I'm hard up and he came. He teases me, confident now, flicking my lower lip with the tip of his tongue.

He is so different than the women I've been with. His mouth is strong, no-nonsense, like he could bruise mine if we kissed too hard.

While Oneida busies herself with the charges, Theo runs a hand across my thigh, along my still rock-hard shaft. I gasp, wincing, almost creaming my pants. "You want...?"

It's so uncharacteristic to hear the uncertainty in his voice. Like he doesn't know what to do. Which makes me laugh, because he has a cock, he knows what to do with one.

"Do you want to stay longer?" I want to cum so bad, but no lie, I am nervous too. I hadn't planned on any of this. My imagination has been my only partner, as far as guys are concerned.

"I don't know if I can afford you." He grins, giddy. I would absolutely fuck him free of charge but that would end my relationship with Oneida. She is very big on no freebies in her house.

"Don't you think I'm worth it?" I tease. He kisses me hard.

"Here you go," Onedia slips her phone with the little square attached between us.

Theo sucks air between his teeth at the price, but signs.

When he looks up, he is again the same old Theo I'd always known. He slouches a little, looking into the middle distance somewhere over my head.

"Yeah, well, this was great. Thanks." He rubs the side of his nose.

Oneida slides in front of me, adjusting Theo's clothes like he's a boy on his way to school. I can't see her face, but he warms into charming good nature and I feel raging jealousy.

What the fuck? I ask myself. It must be the testosterone, the raging hard-on, the tease. But this is business, this is a job. I need to be a professional here.

"Better, yes?" she prompts.

"Thank you, Oneida," he says in sing-song mockery, like a schoolboy getting out of class early.

She slaps him lightly on the face. Playful, but also a warning. "Remember what I have of yours before you get smart on me."

His virginity. His reputation, maybe. His money.

Theo laughs like he isn't sure how to take her. That's good. Oneida needs the upper hand to keep her business running, and I've seen her turn grown men into pudding. I imagine a lot of the guys who rolled through here maybe wanted to treat her like a whore, especially afterward. Oneida somehow always keeps them in line.

"Come again," she smiles at Theo.

Theo laughs, not even looking at me. I'm standing here like a third wheel. A blue-balled third wheel who doesn't know what to do with himself.

"Come on, I'll drive you back," I interrupt, and Oneida throws me a warning glance over her shoulder.

I should excuse myself to the restroom and get rid of my frustration, but instead, I am stubbornly staying in the room, taking Theo home. Oneida's eyes narrow like she thinks I'm going to break one of her rules.

I'm not hoping to start something with him on the car ride home, and that decision's not only about Oneida's rule now that my head has had a moment to clear. A guy like Theo, who thinks he's getting freebies because he's so hot, would never let anyone hear the end of it. I just want to stay angry I guess. Sometimes, I don't get myself.

"Hey, thanks," Theo says to Oneida, and leans down to kiss her, all gentle. "I'll always remember you."

"Oh, you pretty boys." Oneida sounds pleased. She places another playful pat on his pec, like suddenly she wants to touch him a little more.

Fuck me, if Theo ever stopped being an ass, he'd probably get smothered in pussy.

* * *

THE CAR RIDE BACK TO THEO'S IS NOTHING LIKE THE RIDE TO Oneida's— Theo slouches easily in his seat, humming under his breath, dumb smile on his face.

It's me who's all keyed up now. I keep getting these flashes of his mouth against mine. The rough quality of stubble just below his skin as his jaw brushed my cheek. There is a no-bullshit aspect to Theo's masculinity, a scent and roughness to his skin that excites me.

He doesn't say anything and neither do I. Because when I'm not thinking about Theo's body, I'm reminding myself how much Theo is going to hate me when he sees that video of us together.

I can't regret it, because Kit needed that money for her

meds. I tell myself Theo started all this blackmailing Hailey, and all's fair in that kind of game. But I do regret that this is probably the last time Theo will be goofy in front of me, the last time for sure he'll kiss me and groan into my mouth as he cums.

6

THEO

All I can think, when I can think clearly again—

No, screw that. I can't think.

It's a blur, a surge of excitement and newness and horniness and all I can do is grin like a dumbass.

His mouth on mine. Her mouth on me. The moment the rhythms synch and his tongue darts across my bottom lip, so ticklish and intimate, as her tongue slides along the underside of my cock? Thrusting into her mouth, sliding into her as I kissed him?

I'd cum so hard my eardrums stretched like a sonic boom.

And after, I'd slid my hand up his thigh and felt him. I didn't think I cared that he was just doing his job, that this was all about losing my virginity, and I'd gone out in a blaze of glory. But when I felt his cock straining against those fricking sexy black pants, everything in me had tightened with wanting him, the last drops of cum squeezing out of me in a shiver, my head bobbing up for more.

On the way home, I tell myself Lucas— any guy for that

matter— probably gets hard if he's sitting next to someone getting a blow job. That's what I'd been telling myself all the times guys would be talking about fucking and they'd get a rise out of me. It was just part of being a guy. You can't help it.

Except I can't stop thinking about how hard he was.

Before we left, Oneida showed me the added bill— $250 to kiss Lucas, have him hold my hand while I got blown, like I needed some kind of emotional support buddy to spurt down her throat.

I'd told myself it was just fun for me, a cheap charge for a memorable experience. What other guys around here could say their first time was a threesome? Even Jack couldn't say that.

I'd signed off on the credit card slip, aggravated because I knew any minute Lucas was going to get up, excuse himself, and go unload a hot spurt of jizz behind a closed door. It pissed me off to know he was gonna do it for free in the bathroom, when I could just as easily watch. My dick throbbed at the thought.

Oneida must've sensed she could get another round out of me because she started flirting. Can't lie— she's gorgeous– if I'd had the money I might've stayed all night.

"Hey thanks," I'd told Oneida. And then I'd said the stupidest fucking thing: "I'll always remember you."

Which was true, but I sounded like a geeky virgin in love with the first person who'd touched me.

"Come on," Lucas had grabbed the porch door knob, probably aiming to get me out of there before I did some-thing even more cringe-worthy like proposed marriage.

He'd never excused himself to beat off. I could tell he needed to, all his muscles flexed and hard, not at all like Lucas' regular chill attitude. I knew what it was like to have a dick— they might go down, but they were always waiting for any reason to surge again. Lucas' second-hand embarrassment for me swooning over Oneida had been even more pressing than his need to cum.

I'd followed him to his car, practically floating. I couldn't get over how good this felt. I got why Jack, Ella, and Hailey couldn't control themselves, going at each other like farm animals in the back of the beef barn. If I had access to Oneida, to Lucas' mouth, I'd be stuffing my dick at all times into their dark crevices.

* * *

Now, the two of us are alone together in his car.

All I want to do is reach across the car seats and put my hand back on his thigh. I have the advantage now, knowing he's hard up, knowing he's open to kissing me at least.

But you have to understand— one night of success didn't make me invincible. And I have at least a decade of sitting across from dudes and not crossing any boundaries, of fearing what kind of names I'd get called if I got too familiar with the bros at BBall.

I don't want to do anything to ruin tonight. if I get rejected again, I'd be back to who I'd been before. And Lucas might easily reject me. After all, I'd essentially be trying to scam a freebie off him.

Still... his hard-muscled leg flexes as he presses on the brake, the gas. The black pants crumple a bit at his lap. In glances, I think I can make out the outline of cock, and it takes my breath away.

I can't do anything. Can't kiss him, not while he's driving the familiar streets of our town where anyone might see. Instead, I let myself imagine dropping my head down into his lap. I'd exhale, long and slow, against his zipper, warming the parts of him underneath...

How did he get this job? How often have people paid him to do to them what he just did to me?

I don't open my mouth to ask, because, me being me, I'll put my foot right in it. Of course he's done stuff like this before. I just got my card charged for it and nobody besides me batted an eye. And anyway, the real question I want to know is whether he likes me. But if I use some logical freaking reasoning, I know the answer. He's not into me any more than Oneida is. If I'd gotten a tattoo or a massage, I wouldn't think the service people doing that job had the hots for me.

The car moves into my neighborhood, which has muted street lights, heavily domed to create pools of light that never shine directly in anyone's residential windows.Our time is almost up. I know I'm gonna mess it up with words, but I've got to say something before I walk away.

"You ever..." My voice comes out so froggy I have to clear my throat.

Once I tried to cheat off Lucas in a Chemistry class. It was in the middle of Basketball season, and I didn't get to study, and I panicked, using my height to tilt in my chair to see some of his answers because I knew he was a smart guy. Subtly, he'd pushed his paper towards me to help me out, but also, not as subtly, formed a fist around his pencil and extended his middle finger at me.

Now, Lucas raises an eyebrow at me, eyes still on the road, and I get the sense he's gonna flip me off no matter what I say.

"You know, like Pretty Woman..." This is the movie that comes to mind, because I'm an ass. My mom owns a copy and watches it every so often, drinking wine on the couch and ignoring us. Helpless to do anything but continue, I add, "You know, fall for a client?"

Oh shit. I swear, I hear what I sound like. If there was a class in not being an asshole, I'd take it.

Lucas laughs, and there's at least the small relief that he knows me, so me being supremely awkward is not a surprise. Hey, he's even gotten hard for me, knowing who I am. It gives me hope.

"You want me to be your pretty woman?" he asks. I think he's teasing.

"Look." I straighten in my seat. "I got... I got some friends to pony up for my visit tonight." Truth. "And I want to, you know... do that again. But I don't know if I can... and look, I know you were hard. I can..." I fumble into excruciatingly painful awkwardness and give up.

"You can what?" Lucas asks in that neutral way where I'm fairly sure he's messing with me.

I hesitate. Maybe he's really offering. If I say, *I can get you off,* it'll be out there. I'll be all the way out there.

And of course, I have never ever made things better by talking.

"Screw you, man." I scoff like it's a joke.

We are almost back to my house. Lucas is as untouch-able, unreadable, as ever. He pulls into my drive, throws the car in park. He has to want me, want something from me. Or maybe it was just a job for him.

The thought makes me want to touch him even more, make him change his mind.

"I was never on the menu," he says.

"What?"

"You asked if I was on the menu, and the truth is, no. Not for guys."

"Oneida just charged me $250 extra," I practically howl. I

could've negotiated at least. But then the second part hits—he's not on the menu. He's telling me he doesn't do guys.

No. No way I was his first and he was my first.

I lean across the seat and kiss him. I don't really care it's in my driveway. I don't really care if anyone sees. I care that I get to kiss him again.

He kisses me back, hesitant. Then more passionate. Holy shit, I would never have guessed.

He breaks the kiss suddenly and we are both panting.

"Look," he says. "There's something you should know." But then he doesn't say anything.

"I want to see you again." I don't give him time to say no. I can't let him stop this, whatever it is, between us. So I get out of the car and shut the door behind me, saunter up to my front door. I hope he's watching me. I imagine his gaze moving across my shoulders, to my ass, the calves I've worked so hard to perfect.

I hope he's pounding himself through a tight fist right in my driveway because he can't stop once he's alone.

7

Monday means working at Rolling Green all day. Every shift I can get, I take. Even with my side-hustle of literal hustling, I've got to clock hours to make ends meet.

That's fine. Free time leads to things I can't afford: hobbies, love interests, and friendships. I can't afford to let myself care about anything more than I care about family right now. My mother works her ass off to pay bills. Kit's depending on us. They both need my help.

I roll in a few hours before Hailey and get everything prepped at the Snack Shack. I wipe down loungers, tables, and chairs. I empty any trash cans the late shift missed and reline them. I check all the boxes on my worksheet to prove I've done the chores and alert maintenance for anything I can't do myself. I refill the fridge and put in orders to Ron for more hot dogs buns and onion rings. I test the pool water to make sure the chemical balance meets the health code. I run the net around the edge to collect leaves and dead bugs.

I was a High School freshman when I realized I wouldn't

go to college right after graduation. Dad had been gone for a while, but that's when I figured out how bad the money situation was. I'm OK with that. College will be there my whole life. Kit might not be. When you have a little sister who might never get to go to college herself, your dreams merely getting deferred for a few years seems pretty unimportant.

Maybe that's why I have so many fantasies about the doctors at her hospital. I'd already figured it was a way to feel all those horny, romantic teenage feelings while at the same time being safe from ever acting on them. I'd even kind of questioned if maybe the whole liking guys was just another way for me to funnel my fantasies into an impossible scenario — like once I actually experienced a guy, I'd realize I was straight, and having crushes on the medical staff was just another way of never allowing myself to want something that would take me away from my obligations.

But that kiss with Theo? I have to be pretty bisexual because Theo is a cocky bro I'd mocked all through school. If I got wood off him despite being well acquainted with his personality, it had to be because guys are my thing.

Or at least Theo is my thing, for the time being.

Not that it matters. I mean, in a different world, maybe I could have some kind of twisted Pretty Woman situation with him— I needed the money, and I could work out all my sexual repression on him until he was broke. Except I'm pretty sure that in the next week or so, someone is going to show Theo the video we made of him, and Theo is going to show up here and punch my lights out.

I can't blame him. I'd do the same.

You'd think I'd be on edge working at the Snack Shack like a sitting duck, but I'm not. Theo knows where to find me, and there's no way to hide in a town this small. Just like there's no way to change what happened. Might as well accept it.

Hailey comes in around noon, cute as ever. She has what my mom calls 'doe eyes' because they are impossibly big, dark, and liquid. Plus, Hailey always looks at people like she fully trusts them. Today, she has her hair up in a high pony-tail and her face shaded by a green and white Rolling Green visor. Black shorts, and a white shirt.

Hailey has a little jiggle thing going, which mesmerizes the golfers. She doesn't seem to notice how they linger when she's taking orders. There's one old dude who's figured out Hailey will pick up a wrapper if he drops it near the trash instead of in it. He'll watch like one of those old wolf cartoons as she bends over to get it. Hailey doesn't seem to know the effect she has on guys, which makes her alluring but also tends to make guys joke about her. It just seems safe, you know, like she's never gonna figure it out.

"Hi, Lucas!" She gives me a bright smile and a wave as she comes in.

"What gives?" I ask her.

"What do you mean?"

"You. You look... you look really happy, Hails." The last few days she's seemed stressed and sad.

She beams at me, cheeks all shimmery pink. "I am. I mean, I just... It's a great day."

I settle onto the stool and give her a wink before hauling The American Journal of Pediatric Medicine abstracts I drove all the way to State to print out.

"Oh yeah?" I ask Hailey, enjoying the smell of chlorine and sunblock.

She leans into me, barely containing her glee. "Yes. Because I solved my blackmail problem."

My stomach sinks. It doesn't take a genius to connect the

dots. Jack must've threatened Theo to back off Hailey, most likely using the video I helped tape this past weekend. Which means Theo now hates me.

* * *

I GOT THE JOB WITH ONEIDA WHEN I WAS SEVENTEEN.

Until I was legal, she kept me under her wing, showing me how to do the business side. I drove people to her work apartment where she did 'life coaching'. I waited in the walled backyard, hidden from the street, in case she hit the panic button.

If she did, I was supposed to bust in and grab the john, throw him against the wall, and wait for further instructions. Most of my other chores were what you'd expect: changing sheets, doing endless laundry, running the dishwasher, and keeping things tidy.

Oneida and I became friends... or at least more mentor/mentee than mere coworkers. She started coming to the pool to watch me practice flirting with the women there. She'd give me pointers, giving me little tidbits about which women had disposable income, which had husbands who might cause trouble. I started gathering attention at the pool. I knew she was grooming me. I was glad. I needed all the money I could make.

Later I found out Oneida hadn't just chosen me out of the blue. She did it as a favor.

See, my mother is a single parent. My dad's busy drinking away his guilt for not being able to take care of his family. I hope he drinks himself to death. We're better off without him.

My mom co-owns a hair salon, and she works as a caterer on the weekends. She does some tailoring in her free time. She babysits. She drives rich kids to their karate classes after school while their parents are still at work.

Someone told my mother to ask the hospital for an itemized billing, that sometimes doing so could reduce the charge, because they had to prove what they were charging for. Other friends told Mom to apply for drug coupons and ask for samples at the doctors' offices. They told her to make a plea with the board of directors and administrators at the hospital.

I don't know what happened when Mom went in to plea my sister's case in front of the Sierra Vista Hospital Board. I do know she practiced her speech for two weeks, researching, writing on index cards, and rehearsing over and over while she made us breakfast and I cleaned up after.

What I do know is she must've touched someone's cold, greedy heart in some messed-up way. The board voted to give Kit a grant covering $40,000 of her medical care. Which immediately went back into the hospital's coffers to pay off the debt we already owed.

After the meeting, one of the board members approached her and said they could get me a job working as an 'assistant', with greater than minimum wage hours.

I think my mom knew it wasn't on the up and up, but desperate times, man. To be fair, I don't believe she knew I'd be hooking. And to be even more fair, for a whole year in the beginning, I wasn't. It took a while for Oneida to trust me.

When I started bringing extra money home, Mom was so, so, SOOOOO grateful to the board member who'd given her the contact. She sang his praises everywhere she went, and more than once told me how lucky I was to have gotten such a lucrative job because I'd happened to work at Rolling Green, where the board member had noticed me and my 'work ethic'. Who cared that he asked for a 5% kickback of everything I made? Even though he was rich and I was working to save my sister. Even though all my money was going straight back into the hospital where he worked.

You know where I'm going with this, right?

Theo's dad got me the job.

8

———

Lucas

Coaxing smiles out of sunbathers and taking drink orders gives me plenty of time to think about Theo and all the stuff I usually cram in the box I call "Work Stuff, Don't Touch".

I feel like an asshole about the tape and decide I won't do anything like that again. Working in a grey area trade means I've got to have rules so I can look myself in the mirror in the morning, even if refusing some jobs means I make less money, which in turn means less medical care for Kit. Guess I've found blackmail is a fridge too far. But my decision doesn't exactly help Theo.

I decide Theo's dad will fix it— if he could get Oneida to take me on as an employee, he could quash a blackmail attempt on his son. Honestly, I'm a little shocked Oneida allowed the tape to go out since she clearly has some kind of relationship with Theo's dad. But I do know Oneida likes to play games, so there's probably an angle I haven't figured out.

I am totally wrapped up in my own drama when one of

my regulars gets talking to me over an order of Caesar Salad with chicken, no dressing, no croutons. When I look up, I realize that behind the sunglasses, she's weepy, blotting her cheeks with the paper napkin that came with her Diet Coke.

This happens more than you'd guess.

"Hey, let me get that salad for you at no charge," I say.

"Oh no, Lucky." She gives a long sigh.

No secret around the club that my name is Lucas here, but I'm 'Lucky' at Oneida's. I don't like it. There are about a million jokes about a guy whose name rhymes with 'fuck' working with a woman sometimes called O. But Oneida encourages it, says it helps to develop a persona with the customers.

My regular shakes her head adamantly. "Put it on my tab, and let me buy you some lunch too."

"Appreciated, but you know I can't do that."

"I want Hank to pay for your lunch." She lowers her glasses to give me a tear-stained and teeth-bared grin. Hank is her husband, I think.

I wink and punch in her order. No way in hell am I gonna charge my lunch to her account. Clients have a lot of emotional drama— which I completely understand because when they visit me, they are usually going through something— but you could not pay me enough to get me in the middle of it. Any more than I do at O's house.

Except with this unfortunate blackmail video, which I wasn't even supposed to be in but I've allowed myself to get right in the middle of.

Back inside the Shack, I get the order started and head back out with her drink. I hand it to her.

"Do you have time for me?" she asks.

"Of course," I say. "What's good for you?"

As she lists off a date and time, I catch sight of Theo walking down the path from the main entrance.

"I...I'm sorry, what?"

She looks over her shoulder nervously, but also *hopefully*? I think she wants her husband to catch her. "Is everything OK?"

"Yeah, fine. I just... I just had a moment." I make a point of relaxing, focusing on her, making her feel comfortable. Her shoulders come back down.

"I have those too," she flirts.

"Let me call you later," I say. "I'm sure I have time for you."

She blushes, looking guiltily around the pool. I think maybe that's part of the excitement for some of them— worrying about what other people notice, or half hoping their spouse will be there, angry and possessive. No doubt 'Lucky' gets used in this job, and this feels like a somewhat dangerous trick— she's looking for drama and may throw me under the bus to get it.

But that's what the money pays for.

* * *

THE SECOND I'M SURE MY CLIENT WON'T TAKE OFFENSE AT ME hot-tailing it out of there, I hurry from her lounger, hoping Theo hasn't seen me yet.

If I'm going to take a punch or be the receiving end of a shouting match, I know better than to have it happen where everyone can see. My job is an open secret at the club, but the fact that sometimes people get blackmailed at Oneida's definitely isn't, and would definitely mess up the levels of trust I've built with clients.

My flight options: Snack Shack.

Nope. The concrete foundation and open windows only make everything that happens in there louder. Plus Hailey is in there.

Wait, maybe Theo is coming for Hailey. I mean, if he's been blackmailing her and is now getting blackmailed, he may be more pissed at her.

I spin around, trying to gauge where he's headed and who he's most angry at. I can't leave Hailey to defend herself against Theo.

But he's coming for me. Or seems to be. His sunglasses hide his eyes, but I've gotten pretty good at figuring out what people are looking at behind their shades.

Usually, at this place? It's my crotch.

I pause to make sure. Yeah, he's coming for me. There's a smile on his face, but that might be a distraction. I can't tell without seeing his eyes.

I walk past the Snack Shack since I don't want Hailey to get mixed up in this. That leaves Ron's office, the employee locker rooms, the storage shed, and the parking lot. None of those options are floating my boat.

I feel safest in the employee locker rooms, so I head there. If Theo follows me inside, at least it will be on my turf.

Inside, I push the door closed behind me, fighting the pneumatic swing. I don't lock myself in. Theo pounding on the door and shouting accusations won't help.

I take a breath, waiting. Silence. The smell of mildew and sunscreen. Cool air radiates up from the damp concrete floor.

My heart thuds and I glance around to see if anyone else is in here. Nope, I have it all to myself. I turn to face the door, waiting to see if Theo will come in or give up and find me later.

There is a crack of light at the bottom of the door, a long thin triangle of sunshine where the door isn't perfectly hung.

The triangle breaks into three lines. He's right outside.

I want him to come in.

It doesn't make sense. He's probably going to beat the shit out of me, or at least try to. He's going to demand answers or make threats to expose me. He's going to fuck up my business for sure if he starts yelling loud enough. There was absolutely no reason for me to be getting a semi about any of that. But I am.

I clench my hands, open them, clench again. Theo doesn't shout or pound on the door.

The shadow of his feet moves. Bright triangle again. He's leaving.

I reach out and yank the door open.

"You looking for me?" I call. Like an idiot. Like I'm begging for a fight.

"Oh hey." He says it casual, like he hardly cares, like he's run into me on accident. Blood swooshes through my ears, making it hard to hear him say, "Look, you good to talk?"

I stare at him. What is his game? His lopsided smile doesn't make any sense. The only thing I can imagine is that he, too, wants to keep the tape private, and so he's acting aloof until there are no witnesses.

Maybe he doesn't know about it yet.

But that's wishful thinking. If Hailey knew, it's because Jack has the tape, and so she knows she's not gonna get blackmailed any more.

Or at least, that's what I guess. It's difficult to theorize on the fly.

But seeing him there, not hating me? It floods my cheekbones with tingles, my mouth remembering the taste of his. I hold the door open. "Yeah, man. Step into my office."

Even if I'm wrong, what else am I gonna do, make a break for it? Have this fight in front of everyone at the pool?

Theo ducks a little out of habit as he crosses the threshold and becomes a shadow blocking the bright summer sky behind him.

As he comes all the way in, we touch. Just the barest brush of his arm against my chest, but I catch the smell of him. My skin tingles nipples puckering.

I let the door go and it swings closed in that slow, hydraulic way that takes forever. As the last stripe of light disappears and the outside noises muffle, I wait for him to throw a punch or curse me out, or maybe get tearful. I hope he won't beg me to fix it, because that's impossible now.

In the dimness, I hear myself breathing too loud, the sound filling the quiet as our eyes adjust. Theo puts his hands in his shorts pockets, head bent to get in my body space. He takes a step forward, intimidating. The rasp of my breathing takes on a ragged edge, sounding like a fight getting ready to happen.

I straighten my spine and look him in the eye. Or at least where his eyes should be, behind his dark glasses, in the dim room.

He probably can't see more than a shadow in front of him. This gives me hope if he tries to beat my ass. He'll have to catch me first.

"About Saturday." His voice is gravelly.

I swallow in reflex, clench my hands, ready to defend myself. "Yeah?"

"You do that a lot?"

I give him a slow, knowing smile, determined not to let him see how nervous I am. If he's gonna try to embarrass me or shame me for what I'd done? What we'd done together?

.... Or maybe he means the video.

Shit. I have no idea what he's trying to intimidate me about.

Theo moves closer and I have to force myself not to take a step back. He puts a hand flat against the door, barring anyone who might push it open. I am nervous, but my dick is very, very interested. So interested that if Theo comes any closer, he's going to find out all about it.

"What's it to you?" I say, hoping to egg him into telling me what he's actually doing here.

He takes off his sunglasses. His breath against my jawline, feathering down my neck and against my collarbone. My body reacts with a hitch in my exhale I absolutely cannot control, just like I can't help how I lean into him. Something's going to jump off.

Theo moves so close his hips brush my belly, the heaviness of his cock making slow, heavy contact. His thick, dark lashes are lowered so I can't see his expression.

"Maybe I want to hire you," he says.

Outside, the melody of summer— the splash of a kid cannonballing into the pool, the tweet of a lifeguard's whistle. In this dark little funky mildew wonderland, everything I never knew I wanted is somehow unfolding. All I can see is his mouth, his lips as they move. All I can think of is the brand he left on my abdomen when his cock knocked against me.

"Hire me?"

The assurance of his palm against the door. I lean closer, ready to drop to my knees and give him anything he asks for.

Theo pulls back just enough so we don't kiss.

He leans harder against the door, arm muscles flexing, cutting off my only exit. I swallow. His eyes slide down my throat.

"You know how to get pussy," he says. "What if I hired you to give me pointers?"

"Wh—?"

"Like a tutor."

The built-up tension, the fear, the attraction, all break inside me and I laugh. He doesn't know about the tape. He wants dating tips from someone about to bang him for free if he'd take a hint. Somehow, I have another chance with him.

Theo turns his head away and hits the door with his palm so it makes a solid thud that echoes in the empty locker room. "Whatever. Fuck off."

He moves to open the door, shoulders hunching. I grab his arm.

"No, wait." I can't stop laughing even though I want to. I guess I was more scared than I thought... although not of him beating my ass so much as facing that I'd hurt him. "Are you serious?"

But Theo is Theo. He yanks away from me. "Forget it."

"No wait, I just... it surprised me is all. Serious. Stay." I am still grinning even when I manage to stop giggling. I ignore the stab of pain, aware he's talking about me being his wingman, not anything between the two of us. "What exactly did you want to do?"

Theo scowls at the floor. By now I'm fairly sure this isn't a trap, but sometimes that's when the best-laid traps mess you up proper.

"You want me to show you how to get a girl?" I lower my voice. "Or...?" I lean in a little closer.

"Yes!" He jumps on the first offer. "Like a coach, you

know? I've got natural talent, right? Girls like me. But then I mess it up. I just need some pointers, feedback."

Something inside me wilts. But I nod, clearing my throat. OK, realistically, I could use the money. I push out of my mind that sooner or later—probably sooner— Theo's going to get that tape in his inbox and know Oneida and I did him dirty.

"Great!" He slaps me playfully on my shoulder. "I leave for school on September 3rd, so we've got to cram some lessons in, you know what I mean?"

"I'm not... I'm not sure what to... Exactly what do you have in mind?"

I have never done anything like this, and I have no idea what to charge, whether I give Oneida a cut, or what Theo expects me to do. The third is only a few weeks away. So naturally, I try to talk him out of it. "I mean, couldn't you hang out with Jack if you want pointers?"

"Jack doesn't tell me *how* he's doing what he does, and whatever..." he hesitates, then sighs. "Whatever it is, I'm doing it wrong. I really need someone to watch my game and tell me how to improve my technique."

Theo grins, and I feel that attraction zing between us again. He must feel it too. How could he not?

OK, maybe he can't and that's how he's striking out all the time.

I lean in again. I can't help it. His mouth. I'm just going to kiss him and screw the rules about freebies, this is my own time and —

"So, there's this party Thursday night," Theo says. "Come with me, bruh. Watch me operate, give me feedback."

"Yeah sure. And uhh... if there's any reason you want to call it off, let me know," I say, dazed. I mean, he's gonna find out about the tape by Thursday. No way was this little date ever going to really happen.

Theo quirks his eyebrow like he catches my reluctance but smiles.

"Thursday night. This time, I'll pick you up." He swings the door open and walks out. And for once, I'm the guy standing there speechless, heart fluttering, craving more.

9

———

Thursday is both mere days and a lifetime away.

Each afternoon, the burning country club sun rolls overhead, wilting the greens and sapping the energy from Rolling Green guests, until they lie on the loungers as if melted into them. Going to the outdoor shed to grab stuff for the upcoming Pops concert means you've got to squint your eyes when you open the door because of the explosive heat that blows out.

Everything becomes seductive— beads of ice-cold condensation on every glass I hand over, the little tracks of sweat that run down between exposed cleavage, how everyone arches and stretches in the sun, clothing sticking to them.

I wonder at least a dozen times by noon if Theo's seen the tape. Maybe he'll just ghost me. Honestly, I might rather have him try and give me a beat down, just for the closure. Wondering about it is killing me.

I don't ask Hailey about it. But I listened carefully to everything she says, attempting to glean some clue as to what's going on with Jack, who paid for the blackmail tape, and Theo.

Hailey seems blissful— Jack is staying in town, going to the community college.

"I thought he was going to..." I trail off, embarrassed.

Everyone knows Jack had been planning to go to college with Ella. Her dad had made a big to-do about giving his daughter's boyfriend a scholarship. On the surface, it was about Jack being an outstanding employee at Rolling Green, but obviously, it was also straight-up nepotism.

Then Jack had broken up with Ella and gotten fired. Guess his scholarship had died right after his relationship with the boss' daughter had.

Hailey forces a wide, triumphant smile, shaking her head so slightly it's like a tremble. "No, no, he's enrolled at community. We're doing it together. And... and Ella's going back for her sophomore year." Hailey's face goes red.

"Hey, Hails. I don't care," I say gently, to put her out of her misery. And also because I don't really care. This is the advantage of being too busy to get involved with small-town drama.

She bursts out laughing. I think she must feel guilty about dating Jack. She and Ella were pretty chummy this summer. But whatever. I've done more morally reprehensible things this week.

Come to think of it, I haven't seen much of Ella lately, just her popping in and out to sign off on Hailey's time card, usually early in the day before Hailey makes it to work.

I get up to go refresh some drinks. Just as I'm in the bright sunlight again, I catch Ella and Theo walking down a side path from the parking lot to Rolling Green's main building. She says something and he laughs, casually and with genuine good nature. Neither of them so much as glances at the pool area. I burn with jealousy.

He's here, and he's not coming to see me. In fact, he's chasing Ella Stewart while I've been wasting my time obsessing about him. I turn on my heel and go back into the Snack Shack.

Hailey, too, looks shell-shocked. I follow her gaze as she watches Ella and Theo until they disappear into the main building. He holds the door like a real Rolling Green gentleman.

"You OK?" I ask.

She shakes it off. "Yeah, no. I'm just. You know. A little lightheaded, I think?"

I see my chance for info and jump on it. "Theo still giving you trouble?"

She blushes, studies her cuticles. "It's fine," she mumbles.

"Hails, what's going on?"

She looks at me like I've grown another head. "Nothing! Jeez." And then she disappears out the door with a tablet.

Crap.

By Wednesday, I get it into my head that Jack must be holding onto the tape for some reason. It's the only thing I can think of why Theo hasn't shown up pissed off.

I don't understand why anyone would pay for a tape and then not use it, but there are lots of things I don't get. This world is full of secret dramas and soap opera bullshit, up to and including women at the pool getting bored and jealous for my time, or their husbands finding out and coming after me.

What I'm trying to say is that while I was on my guard for Theo to come at me, this wasn't my first rodeo in the revenge games. There are other small fires I had to put out on the daily, and that's not including the ones that pop up about my sister's health or on her color-coded chart of doctors, meds, and insurance forms.

Thursday rolls by, no Theo. What. The. Hell?

That's about when I decide he *does* know I helped tape him at Oneida's, and instead of punching me out, he's taken the road of totally ghosting me. He'll just pretend we never knew each other, and soon enough he'll go off to State for college and I'll stay here in town, and that will be the end. In fact, this is already the end.

Which is when I find myself wishing for an angry Theo. Any kind of Theo sounds better than none. Which is also stupid, because I don't have time for any kind of anything.

It's really better this way, I tell myself.

After work, I pull out my phone, consider texting him.

But I don't. I toss it into the seat next to me and head home. I press my palm against the back of my neck, feeling the radiating heat of the sun baked into my skin. At every stoplight, I glance at the phone to see if there's a text.

At home, I throw my clothes into the hamper, wrap myself in a towel, and head for the shower.

Ghosting is a punishment favored by Rolling Green members, I realize as I consider what my clients through Oneida have told me. Wives married only a few years have told me they haven't had sex with their husbands in six months or more. One told me it started with a cold shoulder fight after a night out at dinner and snowballed into some impassable contest where sex was something you won if you made the other person grovel for it.

I should be glad it's worked out this way. Theo and I weren't really friends, so it's not as though there will be some big hole in my social calendar without him. And his silence leaves my side hustle unexposed. I should be relieved.

I stand under the lukewarm spray of the showerhead. I should be looking forward to the weekend, enjoying the relief of not getting caught, and working to pick up a few new clients at the pool before the Snack Shack closes up for the off-season.

I'm still thinking all these things as Kit monopolizes the dinner conversation with some new flick on Disney Plus, and I offer to clean up the kitchen if Mom wants to go start it with her. Kit cheers and soon the TV is going so loud in the living room I don't notice my texts buzz until the second one comes in.

Theo: *Be there in 20*

Oh shit. That one came in during dinner. And just now,

Theo: *Here. I think. This your address?*

My address is below.

I throw down the washcloth. I'm wearing old jeans and a beat-up T-shirt splashed with dishwater.

Me: *Be right there*

Theo: ....

I curse under my breath, working at light speed to get the last of the dishes in the rack. I scrub a pot like a chore zealot, but I'll have to let a few things soak.

"Ma?" I call over my shoulder. Cartoon characters sing loudly from the living room. "I'm going out. I, uh, I forgot I'd agreed, and they're here now, so I gotta—"

She comes into the kitchen, looking tired and concerned. "What is it?"

"Nothing, Ma. Just a party I said I'd go to and then—"

Her expression lights up. "A party? Go! But not like that. Go change. I'll get the rest of this."

She is so happy to see me go out, it kills me. "Hey, thanks. I'll—"

"Go. Have a good time." She shoos me away. "You're always working... this isn't work is it?"

I head for my room, stripping off the damp shirt. "It's fun, I swear!"

"Good!" she calls after me. She knows I work for Oneida, but she thinks all I do is the muscle for hire stuff. "You deserve it."

10

———

I swing open the front door, still in my rag-tag jeans—they're old but they look good on me, worn to the level of softness only favorite jeans can attain. Besides, I don't have a lot of options. The shirt is one of my favorites.

Theo leans against his car, arms folded, scowling. He's wearing shorts like always, this time cargos that look new and expensive. His T-shirt has a crease down the front as though it is technically brand new.

I jog down the walk to where he stands. "Hey."

He turns away to open his door. "You're late."

When his back is to me, I smirk. Maybe I should've been irritated by his attitude, but what I actually feel is relief— I'd thought I'd never talk to him again.

I sling myself into the passenger seat of his car and pull the door closed. Theo scowls at the dash.

"Well look who's mad as a wet hen," I say in a goofy voice. I can't help it. I am so pleased he actually showed, it's made me giddy.

"I'm not—" Theo scowls.

"Bitter as a pill?" I run right over him.

He looks at me, rolls his eyes, working hard not to smile.

"Pissed as a parrot? Angry as truck nuts?"

"What?" He starts laughing despite himself.

His laughter is contagious, but I manage a, "You mad bro?"

"I don't like waiting," he laughs, lightly punches my shoulder.

"Sorry," I grin. "I didn't see the first text until I got the second. When you pick someone up for a date—"

"This isn't a date." Theo shifts in his seat.

"Yeah, but you hired me as a coach, so I'm telling you, when you pick someone up, you gotta set the time earlier than 'I'm coming over now' so they can be ready. Girls especially, they like to have time. Or, if you just show up, you gotta expect it's gonna take a minute."

Theo stares at the steering wheel, stops, rearranges his face into that of an obedient student. Takes a deep breath. "OK, yeah. I can do that."

This strange chill runs over me. In my experience, people don't change. Just like teachers recycle their same tests every year and so you can make straight As if you get someone to give you their old homework folder, most people act the same over and over again. Theo's handsome, Theo's athletic, and ever since I've known him, Theo's been an asshole. It's never really bothered me— maybe my thing for doctors is actually a fetish for jerks who sometimes act like they are gods. But this thing Theo is doing now? It's new.

"So where are we going?" I ask.

He gives me an extremely cute wink and starts the car.

* * *

We drive, Theo fiddling with the radio as traffic lights glow in the night sky, my sense of excitement growing. Down surface streets and main drags, into the ritzy part of town. He pulls into an old, fancy neighborhood, and a few minutes before he pulls into the drive of a stately mansion, I put two and two together. We were going to Ella's.

"Stay here," he orders as he throws the car into park and bounds out to the elegant front entry of the Stewart house.

Waiting in the car, I get nervous. There is clearly no party going on, and I try to assure myself it isn't a trap. I imagine Mr. Stewart and Theo's dad coming out of the house, followed by police officers. When Ella comes to the door in a pair of lowrider jeans and a crop top that violates all the old school dress code ordinances about being too sexy, I breathe a sigh of relief.

They talk easily under the porchlight, smiling and gesturing.

Maybe Theo just wants some tips for getting together with Ella, and then my job will be done. Honestly, it doesn't look like the two need me— they seem friendly enough. They probably just haven't already gotten together because Jack dated Ella and Theo used to be Jack's best friend.

At least until whatever happened that made Jack pay for blackmail on Theo.

Theo gestures at the car and Ella nods. The two of them come down the walk.

Quickly, I get into the back seat, being a good wingman and all. Ella looks surprised to see me, and I wonder if Theo's second mistake is setting up a date and then making it a threesome.

That word puts me instantly back to the night with Oneida, the way Theo'd opened his mouth wider against mine and groaned as he'd cum.

"M'lady," I say with mock chivalry, gesturing to the empty front passenger seat.

"Hi Lucas," she smiles, unsure. "I didn't know you were coming."

"I can bail."

"No way, loser," Theo slings himself in the driver's seat, his weight rocking the car a little. "You're coming with us."

"Yeah, don't be ridiculous," Ella adds before turning to buckle her seatbelt.

"I thought you two...," I mumble, not understanding at all what tonight's deal is.

Ella laughs. Theo makes a face. "No. Lucas, come on, man. That's my best friend's ex. Ella and I are just friends, right Ellsworth?"

"The best," she says in such a strange way, I'm not sure if she's being super sincere or sarcastic.

I settle back and Theo gives me a look through the rearview mirror that seems to question my expertise. I give him a glance back that suggests, *WTF man?*

He grins. I think he likes keeping me in the dark.

Ella directs Theo out of downtown and into the slightly more run-down, community college area, where students have taken over the old Craftsman bungalows and aged apartments. There are lawn flamingos every third house, and plenty of third-hand couches sitting on front porches.

As Theo turns onto another residential street, music comes from one of the houses and parking becomes impossible. Groups of college kids congregate along the cracked residential sidewalks. Two drunk ones stumble into the road.

"Hey! Move it!" Theo rolls down his window to yell. They laugh. He honks the horn. They flip him off and saunter across the street.

"There," Ella says, although she doesn't need to. "That's it."

"Who's party is this?" I ask.

"Remember Tricia and Brits?"

I nod. They'd been cheerleaders in Ella's year. About a third of our graduating class goes to the community college every year since tuition is free for the first two years. I, myself, am taking classes there. But I only take one or two a quarter, because that's what I can handle with everything else.

Living the charmed life as he does, Theo somehow immediately finds parking, and the three of us walk up to the party house.

"Five bucks each," a guy standing at the doors says. Theo passes him a twenty and gestures at all of us as we walk through. "Keep the change."

Theo pats the guy on the shoulder. Somehow even when Theo's doing something technically nice, he comes off as a douche.

I don't have too much experience with college parties, but right away, the vibe seems way more mellow than high school parties, where everyone's trying to get laid for the very first time or whatever. Most of these college kids look like they've ridden that ride a couple times already. They have slow, knowing faces, eyeing us as we walk into the room. A cloud of smoke hangs at the ceiling, and the house has a greasy feel like it hasn't been cleaned since the people living here signed the lease, but it's comfortable. As I said, mellow.

Theo, naturally, is harshing that mellow. He's tall enough that he hardly needs to get up on tiptoe to see across the room, but he does anyway, frowning at everyone like they are in his way.

"Who you looking for?" I ask. A girl on the couch stretches tall to try and see what he sees. As she does, she spills her drink on the girl sitting next to her. There's some cursing and quick movements.

Theo shrugs. "Just looking."

"Here's a tip," I offer under my breath. "How about looking at what's right here in front of us."

Theo nods like a studious kid, inspecting the room: a pile of college kids on the couch, one getting up to go dry off in the bathroom, a drunk girl in a halter top half-heartedly apologizing, a bunch of red solo cups and beer bottles on the coffee table.

"Hey," Theo says to the room. To my surprise, Halter Top grins at him. Guess Theo's looks go a long way. She launches herself from the couch.

"You look so familiar. Do we know each other?" she asks, stumbling over someone's outstretched legs as she comes closer.

"Probably," Theo says, like *everyone knows me.* "I went to high school here."

"... but you're not *still* in high school, are you?"

"No. I'm going to State this year," Theo brags, and Halter Top smiles. "I was in the class below you."

In the next room, they start playing beer pong.

Halter Top nods. "I thought I remembered you! What's your name again?"

"Theo. Bene—"

"Theo Benedict!" she interrupts, laughing.

"Ella!" Theo says over Halter Top's head. "Hey, come here. Do you remember....?" He gestures at Halter Top.

"Denise," Halter Top says a little sourly.

She eyes Ella, who understood the assignment when she got dressed tonight— everyone's eyes are on her exposed hips, on the way her little top looks like you're gonna catch a glimpse of something you're not supposed to see. Ella's the pinnacle of physical perfection at this party, and everyone, including Ella, knows it.

"Hi, El." Halter Top says, definitely not appreciating having to stand next to Ella. "Look," she says to Theo. "I gotta go pee."

She pushes lightly to get around his frame.

"More than I needed to know!" Theo calls after her. She scowls over her shoulder and heads for the beer pong room.

Theo gives me a perplexed look like, *What'd I do?*

Ella hands me a beer and I drink quickly from it to hide my laugh. Theo has not lied about needing help. Ella hands Theo the other beer but he shakes his head.

"I'm driving remember?" Theo shouts over the cheers of the beer pong players.

"Yeah, we're drunk, not deaf," Ella snaps.

I actually think it's pretty cool, and raise my drink at him in thanks before taking a sip. Ella prances off, obviously enjoying the appreciation and envy she gets from the crowd.

"You like her?" I lean into Theo to dude-whisper in his ear.

He's just tall enough I have to strain a little to do it. I imagine him getting chills as my breath tickles that sweet spot at his neck, by the base of his hairline.

"What, Ella?" Theo screws up his face and shakes his head. "I mean, she's great. *Really* great. She's got my back. But she's..."

She's Jack's girl. She's a bit full of herself. She's too perfect somehow, like she'd always love herself the most.

I think I read these things from Theo's expression. I hope he doesn't read the happiness in mine. I can't help it. I have a crush on this ding-dong.

I nod: *OK. I'll quit asking.*

We follow her into the back room, scoping out the party, full of unfamiliar and half-familiar faces, some indie college music playing.

I kicked back my first beer and grabbed a second, watching Theo work the room. It doesn't take a genius to see why he's striking out. He's really good-looking, and more importantly, he fits the jock stereotype. He'll start out OK, say something half arrogant and friendly. But ultimately, he doesn't make enough eye contact. He doesn't focus on the girl. Then he'll say something stupid.

They get prickly from lack of attention, or confused, and he gets his feelings hurt.

I watch him bomb like... three times in a row. Maybe only two if you don't count Ella. I start to realize good looks are actually *hurting* Theo. People expect him to be suave. They expect him to know the right moves. If he was less handsome, people might see him how I'm starting to—someone who's trying really hard but just doesn't pick up the social cues.

When the two young women standing by the keg-a-rator discretely roll their eyes at each other and excuse themselves, Theo makes the *SEE?!* face at me. I laugh. I can't help it.

Theo grins back, intensely charming in his ability to acknowledge the scorched earth all around him.

11

Lucas

Halfway through my second beer, I'm feeling a bit liberated from sobriety. And I'll be honest, it's amusing to watch Theo get rejected after a whole four years of high school where I imagined him to get anything and anyone he wanted, whenever he wanted. He's hot as hell, standing alone by the keg-a-rator, grinning sheepishly at me, running a hand through his bronzed hair.

Of course, I was hired to study him, it's natural to root for a student. I groan in over-amused sympathy across the room at him.

For a flash, I see Theo look uncertain. My heart lurches. I want to laugh with him, not at him.

I push away from the wall too quick and feel the booze. But I walk over there to reassure him. He watches me prowl over, and I can't help but put a little swagger into my moves, enjoying his eyes on me. I try to focus on how I'm gonna teach this guy to say the right thing, make him good enough that he doesn't fall for the first girl who's goofy enough to put up with his awkwardness. Which makes my tipsy thoughts wonder what exactly I'm getting paid. We never really worked that out. Somehow, I don't mind.

I land against the wall next to him, too close, so that my jeans brush his thigh. He shifts away, and I wince.

"Sorry man," I mutter, tipping the bottle so he knows it's the booze making me off-kilter.

"Did you see that?" Theo leans over to mutter in my ear.

"Oh yeah. Crashed and burned."

He blushes hot red, but I only grin at him as if to say, *You're paying for me to see this.*

"OK, so tell me, what am I doing wrong?"

He leans even closer in, half turning his body toward me to talk low and private against the music. The intimacy of it sends little trails of shivers along the side of my neck closest to him. I swallow.

"OK, try this out. Look at her when she's talking, and when you want to say something witty, shut your mouth and smile instead."

He scowls at me.

To get him started, I motion at a girl who'd been watching us from the makeshift bar in the corner, waiting for an invite.

I give her a friendly wave. Theo mimics my move. I can't trust myself to look at him. The feel of him studying me sends shivers all across my skin. My body sways to brush his, and it's nothing about being drunk and all about needing to feel him.

She comes over, pretty, blushing with pleasure. She looks stone-cold sober to me, fiddling with the solo cup she clutches with both hands.

"Hi," I say. She dips her head, lovely eyes shadowed by thick lashes. "I'm Lucas." I point to Theo. "Theo."

"Peyton." She sips her beer nervously.

"So... who do you know here?" Theo asks.

Peyton shrugs.

I leave it open for Theo to say something else, but he doesn't, and she doesn't and the silence gets hella awkward. She looks over her shoulder for an escape route.

"Hey, are you willing to help us with an experiment?" I say.

Her face brightens, but she also looks a little suspicious. "Maybe. What is it?"

I lean close and say to her, "My friend Theo is terrible at flirting."

"Asshole!" Theo shoves me.

"See?" I grin at her.

She laughs.

"He's never going to get a girl as cute as you, not with his current game. So I wondered if you'd help us out with a little education."

She quirks her eyebrows and smiles, seemingly game. "What do you mean?"

I take a deep breath. "From a girl's perspective, a pretty girl, like you—" Peyton smiles more deeply. "What do they want from a guy who's trying to talk to them?"

She studies both of us, then focuses on Theo, shyly flirtatious. "I don't know if it can be taught. You either have it or you don't."

"Do I have it?" Theo asks.

As the power shifts to her, she seems more confident. "I mean... Maybe? You're cute. Are you an asshole?"

He grins. "Yeah, sometimes."

She laughs again, making a show of studying him. "Honesty. I like it. Why are you an asshole sometimes?"

Reluctantly, I start making plans to exit the situation.

Theo has enough cruising altitude that this might actually take off.

Theo leans back and looks over her head, thinking. "I don't know. Why are you an asshole?" he asked kind of earnestly.

She pulled back sharply. "I'm uh... not an asshole."

"I mean everyone is sometimes, right?" Theo asks, leaning in, sensing too late it's a mass casualty situation.

Without so much as a goodbye, Peyton pushes away and heads for the other room.

"What?" Theo calls after her.

"Dude..."Once I start, I can't stop laughing. "You *are* an asshole."

He collapses against the wall, pinching the bridge of his nose. "Yeah. I know. I just... I thought we had something in common, right? Her calling me an asshole is flirting, but me calling her one ruins everything?"

"OK, so this is easy," I say and hide my amusement behind a sip of beer. "Rule number one, don't be an asshole."

"I'm not trying to—"

"Rule two," I cut him off. "Don't interrupt the instructor. Rule three, keep the conversation 80% on them. People like to talk about themselves, they like to feel as though you're interested in them. And rule four, don't call them assholes right out of the gate. Save that for the third date."

"Serious?"

"No man. Don't *ever* call a girl an asshole."

He nods, studious and giving me a shit-eating grin despite the fact his ego is clearly bruised. Despite Theo being an asshole, or maybe because of it, I like him. I catch a whiff of his cologne, and under that, the smell of his body, and it flashes in my head again— that slippery, warm kiss.

His tongue against my bottom lip, trying to get me to open for him.

I clear my throat. Thinking about that is good, but it always leads to remembering the tape I'd helped make.

When I look up at him, he's studying me intently, those gold-green eyes taking my breath away. I feel myself blush, suddenly nervous he might read my thoughts and know what I've done to him. Or what I want to do to him.

"Maybe I should try something different," he suggests.

"Sure, what are you thinking?"

He shrugs. "I could pretend I'm Jack, you know. Do what Jack would do."

This hits me somewhere tender unexpectedly. "No, man," I say. "Be yourself. You're going to find someone who likes you for who you are. You don't have to fake that."

He studies me, and there's a silence between us that makes my pulse throb throughout my body.

"OK, I'm gonna try again," Theo says, searching the room.

But people are more than just tipsy now, on their way to sloppy drunk. The time for talking has morphed into the time for dancing, hookups, and regrettable choices. The music gets louder over a wave of cheers from the other room.

I open my mouth to explain all these factors to him, that he should shift gears. But then I realize that's way more advanced than a first lesson. So I shrug. "Yeah sure."

It's not like he couldn't use the practice, and I don't imagine he's going to suddenly get lucky after five minutes of basic training. This way, I can spend more time with him.

But Theo doesn't move from the wall, and there are no nearby girls making eye contact. Every girl who was in here saw him bomb anyway.

I say, "Maybe go in and play beer pong."

"I'm not drinking," he reminds me.

"Well, you should show off your height, and you do better as an athlete than a talker. I'm thinking you channel the Strong, Silent Type for a while."

"Really?" he asks in that honest, no-game way of his.

I take a big swig of beer, embarrassed. "Yeah, sure. You look really good, and you're built."

Now it's my turn to feel awkward. What the fuck?

"I'm gonna go get a beer." I push off, make a quick escape.

"You said I should show off my height, right?" Theo says as he follows me.

It's good advice, even if it embarrassed me to say it. Theo walking and not talking draws a lot of attention from the women at the party, drunk or not. As we pass through the room with the music, one tries to dance up on him, but Theo just keeps walking.

It's too crowded and loud for me to point out his mistake. I'm getting how this isn't going to be a quick lesson or two. On the other hand? The feeling that comes along with Theo only having eyes for me is giving making me think about giving him a different kind of lesson entirely.

He shadows me to the keg-a-rator, where I fill a cup and look around. Someone immediately spills beer on my shoes. The music dials up louder.

"Where'd Ella go?" I ask.

"What?" Theo leans down to shout in my ear.

"ELLA," I say into his.

Theo shrugs, pulls out his phone, and texts. Looks around the room, smiles at another girl leaning against the wall. She smiles back, eyes hazed with booze.

"Let's go talk to her." Theo nudges me.

I go with him. How else am I supposed to tutor the guy?

"Hey," Theo bends toward her ear. "My name's Theo."

"Who's your friend?" she asks.

"Lucas." I lean in to introduce myself.

"Hey, wanna play a game of beer pong with me?" she bats her eyelashes.

"Oh uh, thanks, but..." I gesture to Theo. *I'm his wingman,* I try to indicate.

"Oh! You two are together?" she asks.

"No," I shake my head, annoyed by the roar of the music. "What I meant was..." except then I'd have to explain I was Theo's tutor. Being mistaken for his boyfriend was probably less embarrassing.

I glance up at Theo to try and rope him into doing the work of talking to this potential date, but he's studying the keg-a-rator like he's more interested in how it works.

"Excuse me." She slides between us, brushing her breasts fully across me in the process. I guess she's intentionally mistaken my relationship with Theo and is trying to lure me into chasing her.

"OK, what happened there?" Theo asks. It seems once we've acknowledged he totally sucked with women, he wasn't even defensive about it.

I grin, and shake my head. "That might've been my fault."

Theo laughs and punches me playfully on the shoulder. He is so likable when he isn't trying. That's what I should tell him.

"You're so likable when you aren't trying," I say. As soon as I do, I realized I'm drunker than I'd thought.

Theo doesn't say anything, and I wonder if I've crossed a line. He's always been completely clear about wanting to get with girls, except for our one kiss.

I'd been sure that night he'd been completely attracted to me, but as time has passed, it's almost as if it happened in my mind. To be perfectly frank, people come to Oneida's to do things they would never do in their 'real' life. Maybe he was just curious and decided when he tried me, he preferred women. That doesn't stop me from wanting him at all. Which is totally in line with me having the hots for unobtainable guys.

Nervous, I lick my lips and take another swig of beer. Officially, this is work of some kind... even though I don't know exactly what I'm getting paid. I find I don't mind, even though usually the bottom line rules my life. It's been a million years since I went to a party. This is fun.

"You've seen me crash and burn enough times tonight you must have some thoughts," Theo says between beats of loud music.

"I do."

"OK, lay it on me. So I can turn it around and get some action tonight."

"Yeah, OK. But maybe lower the expectations about tonight."

He flushes, but says gamely enough, "That bad, huh?"

I reach out to pat his shoulder consolingly and say into his ear, "When you're good, you are a hundred percent girl magnate. We just gotta work on some stumbling blocks."

As I pull him in to talk, my hand slides casually up his shoulder and my fingers curl around the nape of his neck.

Catching myself, I step back, letting go. It's getting late. Whatever I feel for Theo, he definitely has a one-track mind about finding a girl. This is been fun, but I'm ready to go. We should give Ella a ride home.

I pull out my phone to text her.

Theo says, "OK, let's go."

He starts walking through the house. I follow, twisting through people. He's easy to spot, being a head taller than everyone else. Through the party, to the kitchen, through a mudroom, to a heavy door I assume leads to the garage. Out he goes.

I'm baffled. This isn't the way to the car, and I highly doubt Ella's here— hardly anyone was in the kitchen and nobody in the little walk-through laundry/mudroom. But I'm game, so I follow him out.

12

———

LUCAS

It's dark, but it smells like a garage for sure. I reach for the wall and find the light switch. Yeah, it's a garage all right, too crammed with stuff to fit a car. Someone's put another couch in here, somehow even older than the one inside. It's pushed against the wall and surrounded by junk— boxes, bikes, a washer and dryer. There's a mini-fridge and a TV a few feet in front of the couch and perched on cinder blocks, a second living room.

Theo squints. "I don't like the overheads."

He hits the garage door opener. With a dusty creak, the garage opens to the street. He reaches over and flicks the lights switch off. With the whole wall open to the street, it's actually really nice— private, but also open. Dark, but the neighborhood lights make for a great view. Of course, it feels super intimate to be in here with Theo, but I'm not sure if that's because I'm drunk and I want him, or if I should trust, as I've seen all night, that Theo doesn't have enough game to think of getting me alone in the dark.

He sighs, flopping on the dusty couch. "Tell me every-thing. Every stupid, asshole thing I did."

"Theo, you weren't really—"

"You can't help me if you don't tell me what I'm doing wrong."

The bass of a new song comes on and I wonder if someone will come out, how long this time with Theo will last. The dark-ness is soothing and pleasant, the breeze the perfect tempera-ture, like a caress. A couple exits the party from the front door and stumbles down the drive, not once looking in at us.

"OK.... " There's so much, I'm a little perplexed about where to start. "So lots of these things are just little cues, you know. It's a vibe. It's—"

My eyes adjust to Theo looking at me as though I'm speaking another language. I wonder if he's ever been tagged for some kind of spectrum diagnosis.

"OK, for example, girls like eye contact, to know you're interested. But not too much, or you'll look like a stalker." I struggle, frustrated. "It's hard to explain."

"Then show me," he says.

"Like what, you be the girl and I show you? Or—" I laugh, tossing my head back, tingles shivering down my neck. For a moment, there is a weird blur and I *am* role-playing— as the flirtatious, nervous girl alone in the dark with Theo. But I'm also myself.

"Either way. Just chose and show me what to do. I'll time it out." He pulls out his phone. Holy... he's got the stopwatch function set up.

I take the last swig of beer and set the cup at my feet, clearing my throat. "OK, say you've gotten to this stage, alone in the garage. And you're talking. What are we talking about?"

"Basketball?" he ventures.

"Sure. As long as it's 80% about her. How are you going to do that?"

Theo rolls his eyes. "So we're talking about TikToks."

"Great. You're sharing them, so you have a reason to sit close, look at the same thing."

There's a weird moment. I am still standing. He's on the couch. If we're roleplaying this...

Hesitantly, I sit down next to him, adjust the lumpy couch cushions, until we are as close as I'd get to a girl I liked— knees brushing.

"Maybe it's time to talk about what I should be charging you for this," I say to break the tension.

"Two fifty," he says like he's thought about it.

I squint. "I got paid two fifty for one kiss. This is a whole night."

He grins. "Yeah, but this is a tutorial. That's like... fifty bucks an hour."

"OK," I agree. "So look at the distance between our knees." I move my leg back. "Friendly." Move it an inch closer. "Flirtatious." Move it until they brush, sending goose-bumps across my skin. "Romantic."

"Show me again," Theo says.

I do. He nods, studious. I set my leg back to flirtatious.

"Start here, so she knows you're interested. Watch her leg. She'll pull back if she doesn't want to flirt. And this is important: You don't go to romantic without some kind of cue from her. And, you don't keep trying to make the distance flirtatious if she pulls back."

"Got it." He practices moving his leg towards and away from mine.

"So now you want to look at her whenever she's talking.

The person who's talking can look around, but the person listening watches."

Theo follows instruction and watches me intently as I speak. In the sunlight, he's got goldish-greenish eyes. Now they are dark, focused.

"You can look at her mouth too, a little, when she's talking," I say.

His gaze dips to my mouth. My cock swells. I shift slightly to hide it.

"So what would be a cue to go to romantic leg?" he asks, all business. He couldn't be more studious without taking notes.

I lean in and put my mouth on his.

I don't plan it. I just want to taste him again. He leans in, kissing me back, his weight pushing me into the couch, my ankle hitting the empty beer cup. It rolls on the cement floor.

Theo leverages his weight so he's so far over me he's practically on top of me but not touching, not crushing me into the couch. I want him to. We are both breathless. I refrain from making a joke about romantic leg and how this is a dozen steps beyond.

"How do I get from this to her blowing me?" He pulls only the slightest bit back to ask.

I laugh despite myself, despite the situation. I know everyone else thinks Theo's an asshole with his inappropriate hot takes, but honestly, he's funny to me.

He pulls back, unsure.

I raise up on my elbows. "Remember the thing about strong and silent?"

He rolls his eyes and leans in to kiss me again. "How much is this gonna cost me?"

"A million bucks," I deadpan.

"Reasonable," he says after pretending to consider.

I punch him lightly in the solar plexus and he falls on me. The weight of him on top of me takes my breath away, and I kiss him hard. I am going to dry hump Theo Benedict in an open garage at a party and I don't care. All I care about is cumming against him, of feeling his mouth groan against me.

"For a million bucks, you should blow me." He wrestles, half tickling, half groping me, and I laugh to cover the fact that I am close to spilling seed while Theo seems to think this is nothing more than practice.

I try to kiss him again, to get what I want, but Theo's fully in bro mode, frustrating my every attempt. I lettered in wrestling, so even though he starts out on top of me, I twist, pushing him into the couch cushions until I get on top, pinning him. He's maybe testing the boundaries of what he can do to me, and I want him to know I take care of myself. He flails against me, powerful, but I don't let go.

"Uncle?" I breathe in his ear.

A group of laughing college kids pass by the open garage, startling me. I let go quick. Theo escapes, kneeling dominant over me. He grabs my shirt neck, twists the fabric in his hand, and pushes me deep into the couch. I can feel his cock against me, hard and heavy. Jesus, he's huge.

We both go still.

"Don't move," he says.

I nod, unable to breathe from wanting him.

He jumps off me with easy grace and jogs to the door. For a moment, I think he's leaving, and I reach out, not sure what to say.

He hits the garage door.

It goes down with a loud, grating rumble. As the light

from outside narrows, Theo jumps back onto the couch, onto me.

The garage goes completely dark.

He lies on top of me, grinding his cock into my thigh as he stretches out over me, and kisses me hard.

I don't ask him what we're doing. I kiss him back, snaking my hands under his t-shirt, ripping it off over his head. This is a party. Someone will come through that mudroom door and see us. I don't care. I don't care. I don't...

Theo runs his hands through my hair as he kisses me, massaging my scalp. He dry humps me with this slow, deliberate, horny rhythm, cock nudging against me, pushing up my shirt as if burrowing into the warmth of my abs.

It's adolescent and awkward, but it feels so good I groan. I reach down and undo my fly, pull my jeans apart and down just enough so that my dick isn't trapped in denim. The change in texture makes me groan again as my underwear hooded cock grinds against Theo's muscled frame, his shorts, the warmth of his body.

I wince.

"What?" Theo goes still with panting effort. I make a note to tell him that's what girls like. They like when you pay attention to how they're doing, that you stop when they signal discomfort.

"You're zipper," I whisper. "It's..." *digging into me.*

"Take them off." He lifts up so I can. "Is that OK?"

I kiss him to let him know it's exactly what I want, and undo his zipper, pulling it open wide and dragging the band of his shorts down around his ass, careful to free his cock from the cargo shorts. He is huge, his underwear stretched over a monster. Before I can get my hand around him, he falls back onto me, like he can't get enough of the way I feel.

He isn't like a woman at all. Not soft, not supple. The

lines of his abs are hard and unrelenting, his skin thick and masculine and strong. We grind slowly, kissing. There is nothing timid about Theo. Like everything else, he puts it out there, wanting me with this unabashed, eager interest.

He bites my lip, drawing me into my mouth, and tilts his hips so the length of his cock slides along my belly. I free him from his underwear, my thumb rolling over his head, feeling the bead of precum. He is desperate and turned on and I have no doubt that he'll cream all over my belly if we keep this up.

"That night at O's, did you?" he says. "Think of me after?"

My balls squeeze at the thought and I have to go still to keep from embarrassing myself. Maybe I shouldn't worry so much about Theo cumming too early.

"Yeah," I admit.

"When you came?"

I dip my tongue into his open mouth, tasting him, and hump against him, desperate for more contact. He grinds into me, his cock sliding heavy and hard along my stomach, his thighs flexing between mine, rubbing against my cock in a way that's pushing me relentlessly over the edge.

"How much for you to suck me off right now," he groans.

"What?"

"A million bucks." He must still think he's dirty talking to me.

"I'm not a whore," I say, which isn't technically the truth.

We both go still, panting. I mean, isn't he paying me for this? I let it get this far, why am I mad at him for assuming I was for sale in this situation when I've been for sale for him before? I don't understand who I'm pissed off at— him or myself. Shit.

"I just..." He pulls back. "Frick, *of course* I messed up."

Except he can't seem to resist dipping down to kiss me

once more, and I can't resist kissing him back, and soon we are grinding again, the couch creaking under us.

"Make it up to me," I pant.

The head of my cock has been poking out of my underwear for a little while now, rubbing skin against skin, precum easing the slide between us. I know he feels it.

"OK," Theo says, with no hesitation.

He grinds even harder into me. *He's a virgin,* I think and almost cum all over both of us. Jesus, I am so wound up for this guy.

Half drunkenly, I tell myself it doesn't matter if I make a fool of myself. He's gonna hate me soon enough anyway.

He starts kissing down my neck. But now that I've thought about the tape, I have feelings. Shitty, guilty feelings. I don't want to hurt him more than I already have. It makes me groan out loud to say it, but I do. "Maybe we should hold off."

His tongue traces along my throat, and he's yanking at my shirt.

I twist like I'm gonna go head to toe with him. "I'll show you," I say.

"I don't know man, that's pretty gay," he laughs.

"What?" I ask back, breathless because I'm so wound up. All I can think about is his mouth, his tongue on my neck, and what it would feel like along my dick.

"OK, but if we do this, no homo," Theo says.

I can't stop laughing. He pinches my nipple and I wince... but still, I can't stop. Maybe under his terrible social skills, Theo's kind of funny.

"No homo," I promise solemnly, my voice bottoming out with desire and the effort not to laugh again.

He kisses me. Whatever else Theo is, physically he's a

god. His abs flex as he nudges his cock into any soft place on me it'll slide against.

"OK, show me how," he says.

If this is part of the lesson I'm teaching Theo, I am in fact, his whore right now. We never set a price, and honestly, I would be doing all this for free.

But if we are doing this for free, I should be honest with him about how he's gonna hate me later.

"Theo, I..." I want to be honest. I really don't want this to stop. He kisses me.

Fuck it. I know better. But two beers and a raging hard-on get the better of me.

We move awkwardly around each other on the couch, shuffling out of our pants, erections springing out of our underwear, his burning like a brand across my skin as we end up side by side on the couch. I grab it, squeeze, testing. Jesus, he's so thick. He works himself through my grasp. All I want to do is taste him.

There's barely enough room for either of us here, and Theo's legs are awkwardly over the edge of the armrest, and there's no lock on our side of the door. And of course, we are two guys about to trade what we are telling ourselves are educational, no-homo, blow jobs.

It crosses my mind that it might even be a set up. Maybe Theo has seen the tape. Maybe he doesn't get mad, he gets even. Maybe I'm about to be the next video to go viral through our friend network.

I don't care. When I feel his breath against my sack, feel him gently pulling it this way and that, inspecting the weight, I decide I would do this on stage if it meant I got what was coming next. My eyes are so warm in my skull that it feels like a fever, and I slide his underwear further down his thighs, bury my face between them, smell him. I have never been this close to a dick, not even my own.

Theo goes still. His breath is a series of quick intakes.

I know the equipment, my own at least, but this is all upside down and backward. I lay my tongue against his head and slowly wiggle it down his shaft.

He groans, moving like he's fucking. It sends a charge through me. My balls go tight.

And then his mouth, warm and wet on me, pulls my cock into him. I couldn't stop myself now if the entire party came through the garage door, flipped the lights, and sang Happy Birthday. I take the head of his cock into my mouth, sliding all the way down the length of him until I almost gag. I move there, slowly.

His tongue swirls along my head, caressing down to the base of my cock. We start grinding again, him fucking my mouth and me fucking his. He gets so deep inside me that I nearly gag, but I don't care. Everything I do, I feel how it turns him on, how he moves faster, more insistently, demanding more or me.

Outside, the muffled music of the party, a cheer of beer pong.

A glass-packed muffler roars down the residential street.

I think the cops will be here soon. I think the door will open. I think the light will flip on and someone will catch us wildly humping on the couch, slick and sliding into each other. All those things only turn me on more. We are going fast and furious, trying to cum before we get caught.

It's building in me, I also don't want to cum because then this moment will stop, and this is bar-none the best sex I've ever had. I pump and pump and pump, sucking him off to show him exactly how I want him to do it, to let him know

I'm almost there, that I can't stop now and I wouldn't if I could.

Theo grabs my ass, fingers digging into my cheek to hold me steady as he takes me all the way down his throat, and it happens.

My balls squeeze and I spurt, everything in me going tense. I make a noise, groaning against him, massaging him furiously with my tongue. He tries to pull away, but I wrap my arm around his ass and he surrenders, thrusting deep inside me until I choke on his cum.

I taste it everywhere. He spurts once, twice, three times, covering the back of my throat, the smell of him filling my nose, the sensation making me swallow reflexively, squeezing the head of his cock with my throat muscles. He groans, thrusting with jagged, strained moves, trying to get farther inside me. Then relaxes.

I pull back, panting, too sensitive to be touched, even though he tries tongue bathing my still rigid cock.

When our panting slows, he tugs at his shorts to pull them up, as if someone walking in now wouldn't understand what had happened here. I lay nestled against his thighs, and neither of us say anything. I couldn't even if I tried. I am rocked to my core. I don't ever want to leave.

Theo's head rests on my inner thigh, heavy, and his breathing evens out.

We should get up. At minimum, get dressed so there would be some semblance of an excuse that we were just drunk and passed out while talking. No one will believe that, but in this town, there are plenty of things that pass for 'the truth'.

Working for Oneida has taught me that.

I'm still a little buzzed, and when he shifts to pull my

shorts up and then nestles against me again, I realize I don't care if the world knows we did this. This feels really right.

I wake up with a headache, shivering, and alone. Theo's gone. Party's over. I'm still in someone's garage. Two hundred dollars falls out of my jeans pocket when I grab them off the floor. I stare at the bills for a long time, but in the end, I pick them up. It *is* money, after all.

13

———

THEO

I am wide awake, body rocking with post-orgasm release. Lucas sleeping against me. My mouth tastes acidic, the strong, musky smell of Lucas' load against my tonsils. I swallow and swallow, but I can't quite escape it. It's a sharp reminder, just in case I forget what we did. What we just did.

Fuck. I said I'd pay a million dollars to do this, and while I know from previous experience, it's not quite that pricy, I am fully aware that just putting my tongue in Lucas' mouth cost $250, and I suspect putting my dick in it is a somewhat higher charge. Lucas meanwhile, is snoring softly into my crotch.

I try to do the math, but for the first time, numbers don't make much sense to me. I gotta figure he costs about the same as Oneida— $1500 for oral. But maybe I worked off some of the cost by sucking his dick? That might make it an even trade. Or... maybe it costs *more*. I've never heard of someone visiting a sex worker and striking a deal that involves no money. That defeats the whole purpose of working for sex.

I honestly have no idea, and when I tried to ask Lucas before, he seemed pretty touchy about it.

Thinking about all this worries me, but my dick is not worried about it at all. In fact, my dick is acting like a trophy wife. As in: dying to spend all my hard-earned cash and make me do stupid stuff for its benefit.

So while I'm sitting here wondering how I get Lucas's snoring face out of my lap and settle up, my dick swells. Despite having shot off a load less than half an hour ago, I can't quite help the hip flex of nudging against Lucas. He feels so good, I groan, doing it again, hand sliding up to clutch his ass and nuzzle my face against him.

Lucas lets out another snore. Not a fake one either. At least, I don't think it's fake.

In a moment, my insecurities join with my math skills, and I realize I am in a terrible position. All I want to do is be near Lucas, but I'm not made of money. And it crushes me to realize all the time we were in high school, he never hit on me before. And of course, I paid him to kiss me. All this... this amazing thing that happened on a filthy couch? This memory that is going in the spank bank until I'm an old man? It's all fake.

I cringe. I even told Lucas that's what we were going to do tonight. He was going to come with me and educate me. He probably thought I meant literally cum. And to be fair, it turns out I did.

I slide off the couch to put my shorts on and check my wallet. I have $200. I hesitate. I don't want to rip Lucas off. I know $200 doesn't cover it. But I want him to know I know it's not a freebie.

"Hey Lucas," I nudge him.

"Nusfwater," he says.

Lucas has these arched, thick, dark eyebrows that can

make his expression humorous or unapproachable in a twitch. Wide mouth, lips not babyish or pouty, but full, sensual, strong, and sure. There is something about him that reads sexy no matter what he's doing.

With an index finger, I gently pull his lower lip down and take a peek at his white squared-off teeth. The tip of my finger grazes them, getting wet. Instinctively, I touch my finger to my mouth and taste him again.

The sweet fragrance of his mouth with a cum chaser. I swallow. The aftertaste remains.

My phone buzzes.

Ella: *Where are you?*

Ella: *The party's kicked*

Ella: *If you left without me, I will make you sorry*

I smile, text her I'm still here.

Ella: *Where?*

I realize she'll start combing the house, looking for me. Shit. I bend and rearrange Lucas' clothes so he looks a bit more proper, but his jeans are still on the floor. I put them on the couch next to him.

"I'm gonna go talk to Ella," I say.

"OK," Lucas sighs.

"Your pants are right here," I add. Lucas snuggles them. "Hey, wake up," I order.

He half sits, squinting. His shirt's pulled up and I see all that tan skin, muscled and smooth. "Yeah, got it."

I'm not sure he's got it at all, but I've started the stupid countdown of Ella tracking me.

"I'll see you later," I say.

It's not that I don't want Ella to know about me and Lucas, although it's so new I *do* want some time to sort out how I feel in private. But mostly, it's that Ella knows I paid to go to Oneida's. Seeing as I've never gotten laid and suddenly

I'm getting head at a house party, I surmise she might guess about Lucas' connection to Oneida. Maybe it's overcautious, but I don't want to put Lucas in jeopardy or hurt him in any way. So you know... I get the frick out of there before she can find me.

* * *

Despite Ella's assessment, the party is still throbbing with music, although there are fewer people, the people who are here look pretty wasted. Someone's fighting in the kitchen, and the floor is sticky. I blink, wanting to leave immediately.

A guy and girl making out next to the door look at me like I've grown a second head. "Hey, I don't think anyone's allowed out there?"

"You're not," I growl, trying to look like I have any kind of authority. Being a tall asshole often helps. The guy raises his arms like I'm robbing him. I add, "It's private. Stay out."

I stand there until they leave. Then I go look for Ella.

"Ugh!" Ella shoves me before I even see her. She is dainty and vicious. "I have been so bored. Where have you been?"

"With Lucas," I say. "Why are *you* bored? These are your friends."

"I thought Jack would be here," she whines. "Didn't he tell you he was coming tonight?"

Had he? I couldn't remember. Honestly, since the whole blackmail thing, Jack and I haven't exactly synced our social engagement calendars. I probably would've gone and apologized except I've been wrapped up in Lucas.

"You know him better than I do," I leer, thinking of the tape. She makes a face and smacks my shoulder again.

"Stop that," she complains.

"*You* stop that," I rub my twice-punched arm. Girls like Ella think they are delicate, fragile specimens and so it doesn't count when they hit a guy. But I'm here to tell you it hurts.

"Hey, will you take me home?" she makes big, sad eyes at me.

I think of Lucas. Ella will follow me like a shadow, and I *did* leave Lucas pants-less in the garage. I don't mind Ella knowing what we did, but I think of how I ruin every potential dating relationship by talking. Ella will definitely have questions that she will ask right in front of him.

I could drop off Ella and then come back for him.

"Yeah, sure," I agree, pulling out my phone. I text Lucas.

Me: *I'll be back. Taking Ella home.*

No response. He probably won't even know I'm gone.

Ella and I, shoulder to shoulder, make our way through the crowd. OK, she might have a point that in the main room it IS winding down, people drunkenly hooking up or passed out. I check my phone again. 1:15

Nothing good ever happens after 1:30, my mother likes to warn me when I'm going out for the night.

It'll take 20 minutes round trip to drop off Ella.

Ella and I drive off in my car, and people see. As much as I like what happened with Lucas, I also like that people see how I'm with the prettiest, most influential girl in our town.

Even if she looks annoyed to be with me.

* * *

"STILL KEEPING THAT STUPID VIDEO TO YOURSELF?" ELLA breaks the silence of our drive to her house.

"Hey, you were a great best friend tonight," I say.

"I would've been your friend without the blackmail," she says quietly.

Even I know this is only half true. We'd always been friends. But now, we have a connection. A bond. But Lucas had said that 80% listening thing, and so instead of arguing with her, I try to think of a question to get her talking. Finally, I just say what I really want to know about her.

"How'd you three get in a threesome?"

"Theo!" she gasps, face going pink and shiny.

I grip the steering wheel. Frick. I'm so bad at this. But I push on. "Come on. How does that even happen?"

Ella studies her pretty, manicured hands and looks like she's gonna cry. Double frick. "I didn't mean to embarrass you, I'm just insanely curious."

In a subdued tone, she says, "Jack said you asked him too. That you offered to trade the tape for the story of how we..."

I nod.

"That's gross," she informs me in a haughty tone and looks out the window.

"Why?"

"Because it's private!"

"Not if it's love."

She whips her head around to eyeball me, incredulous. "Theo, you are just..." She laughs but I can tell she's still mad.

I shrug. "I don't make the rules, but that's what everyone says. If you're kissing and telling, sure that's gross. But if it's love, that's OK to talk about."

She stares at me for a long time, bug-eyed. I catch it in glances between watching the road. On my third or fourth check-in, she's got a strange, embarrassed smile on her face. "Oh. I thought you wanted to know what we..."

"Like, how you met, how you knew you liked each other. I'm not a perv." I make a face at her. People always think the worst of me somehow. "Who made the first move, what they said or whatever."

"What if I said it *was* love?"

Lucas is apparently right about the 80% listening thing.

"Would you call me a dyke?" she asks very quietly.

"I'd be jealous."

"It doesn't matter," she sighs. "It's over." She looks out the window again, all the energy-draining from her voice. "Yeah. Pretty sure it's over."

"Oh." Frick. I'm afraid to say anything. I don't want to hurt her.

But I'm still dying of curiosity. Plus, I'm pulling into her neighborhood. Crap. Even though he starts out on top of me,

"He's going to community college with her. Instead of going to school with me," she says.

"Ellsworth, that sucks."

She sniffles, then laughs. "So if I tell you all about it, will you erase the video?"

I bristle. I thought we were actually being friends. Tonight was probably going so smoothly because Ella has been bullshitting me trying to get me to do what she wants.

"I'm not embarrassed," she says suddenly, defiant.

"Why would you be?"

She rolls her eyes and sniffles. But the next time I glance over at her, she's smiling a little.

"It's shitty to blackmail someone over who they love, just because other people don't get it," she informs me. "And I'm not going to be a part of doing that to anyone. Not even you, loser."

"What does that mean?" I ask.

She opens her mouth, closes it. "It means I'm actually being your friend."

I don't get her. But me not getting social interactions isn't anything new. After a while, I say the only thing I can think of. "Well... thanks."

She doesn't say anything, and I don't say anything, and I drop her off at her house.

All the way back to the party, I think of how Ella said she was in love with them, and how sweet and true it sounded. Totally unlike Ella.

14

———————

Lucas

I wake up in my own bed Saturday morning, happy.

Not exhausted, not worried, not wondering how I'm going to fit all of the day's work into the next twelve hours. Not thinking about Kit's upcoming appointments or the latest research on her condition.

I stretch, my whole body heavy and supple. Bit by bit, the best parts float through my head. Theo. What we did. How he'd clawed my thighs. How I'd arched my back until he'd taken all of me.

And then the not-so-great memories: The money. Walking around the dying party and realizing he was gone. Going out to the street to confirm his car was missing. Having to ask, and one of the party-goers recalling Ella and Theo "Just left. You like literally missed them by five minutes."

Trying to pretend I didn't care.

Even if I hadn't had the best experience in my life with Theo, it would've stung to get ditched by two friends, left at a party.

I reach over and check my phone. There are texts from him.

Theo: *I'll be back. Taking Ella home.*

Theo: *Hey, where are you?*

Theo: *OK, someone said you left. Look*

Theo: *I had a really great time with you.*

My heart flutters. He'd tried to come back for me, I'd just missed him. I totally get him dropping Ella off so we'd have the rest of the night together.

If anyone saw me right now, I'd feel like an idiot because I can't stop smiling, reading the text over and over:

I had a really *great* time with you.

I had a *really* great time with you.

With *you*. *With* you.

I sigh, relaxing into the bed. I like Theo Benedict. I like everything about him. I even like how he can't help but put his foot in his mouth every other sentence. I like how he looks at me when I don't put up with his bullshit. I like him.

I hold the phone up to check if he's texted in the last fifteen seconds. I reread his old texts again. Only this time, I remember the $200 in my pocket and begin to doubt. Lots of clients said things exactly like, "I had a great time". Basically, a thank you for services rendered. A politeness. A dismissal.

Maybe this could work anyway, I tell myself. Theo mentioned a Pretty Woman scenario to me. Maybe that kind of thing would be perfect— he pays, I fall in love with him, we never have the complication of a relationship. o

My heart flutters uncontrollably, and I don't know if I'm miserable at this idea or excited.

Before I can figure it out, the other red buttons at the bottom of the screen finally get my attention. Calls from...

Oh shit, three calls from Mom. A message. "Lucas? I hate

to do this, but Kit's got an early appointment and I got rescheduled. Is there any way you could..."

I jump from the bed, throwing on clothes, checking the time, curse.

"Hey Kit!" I yell through the wall. "Hey, get up, we're late!"

* * *

KIT AND I ARE THIRTY MINUTES LATE TO HER APPOINTMENT.

You don't know what being an asshole feels like until you stand up the doctors who sneak you endless trial dosages of expensive meds. I apologize about a dozen times, and the receptionist tells me if I want to wait, they may be able to squeeze us in.

Kit and I wait for a few hours.

There's a McDonald's up on the main floor, but we've been to this hospital enough to know there's a boring old cafeteria the staff use downstairs. I take Kit and buy her a healthy breakfast amongst tired-eyed staff.

"So where were you last night?" Kit asks over her oatmeal.

I rub my eyes. "Party."

"Was it good?" she asks.

"Yeah," I make a face. "Yeah, it was pretty good."

"Did you meet someone?"

This wakes me up. "What makes you say that?"

She shrugs.

"Come on," I nudge her, trying to pry her into a conversation.

She studies her oatmeal, considering. Then she grins mischievously at me. "Because you're not scoping the doctors."

"I do NOT scope doctors." Most people can't give me shit, but Kit has me blushing hard.

"Not today, anyway," she sasses. "So who is he?"

"No one."

"She?" She raises an eyebrow.

I lean over the table. "Look, I'm sorry I made us late. I won't do it again."

She frowns.

"I promise," I say, sweating a little. I get why she's asking — one night out having fun and I dropped the ball. Now we're wasting our day hoping someone has five minutes to see us. Her health is on the line, and I put my own horniness ahead of that.

She tilts her head. "Why would you promise?"

"Because... Look, I'm sorry. It won't happen again."

"Who was it?" she asks, curious. When I don't answer, she flicks a little oatmeal off her spoon at me.

"Hey!" I jump back. "Quit it!"

"Tell me!" she says. "Tell me tell me tell me!"

"What is up with you?!" I laugh, unsettled, brushing a glop of oatmeal off my forearm.

"Look, do you know how much it sucks that everyone's life revolves around me?" She doesn't say it dramatically, just like a question. Still, it knocks me flat.

"Kit, I love you."

"Then let's talk about something besides me, besides this hospital, besides... ugh, anything. I'm so sick of this."

Her eyes get shimmery with tears. Immediately, I am around the table and sitting next to her, wrapping my arms around her.

"Hey, it's OK," I soothe. "We just got a rough start this morning, running around late, and I goofed it up, and now we've got to wait, but that's OK. That's all this is."

I know it's more than that. It's the day after day, the boredom, the stress, the not being like the other kids. She lets herself cry for three big breaths then wipes her eyes. She leans against me.

I don't care that there's a cafeteria full of medical workers around us. They've seen worse.

"Please tell me," Kit says. "I just want to talk about something."

I smile into her hair. "So there's this guy," I say.

And of course, I don't tell her the Oneida part, or the sex part, or the part about how I'm realizing Theo will leave for college in a few weeks so even if I wanted to have a life, a real relationship with him is a pipe dream. But I do tell her all the good parts, like how I really, really like him.

And by the time they text me that the doctor can see us, Kit is smiling and asking me every question under the earth about Theo.

15

─────

THEO

I wake up to Mom dumping moving boxes right inside my bedroom door. "Morning sunshine," she says, sounding hung-over to the point of near sarcasm.

"Morning," I say into my pillow. "Will you make me pancakes?"

She laughs as an answer. Guess it's cereal. "I want you to start packing up your room today. Anything you're not taking to school, either donate, toss, or pack up for the attic."

I look around at all the sports trophies, the posters. "Can't I leave it here? I'll be back for Thanksgiving, Christmas..." A strange thrill goes through me. I am leaving. I'm not going to see Lucas.

But then: I'll be back, and he'll be here, and we can do stuff to each other again and again and again.

"I've got big plans for this room," she says, pointing to the far wall. "New, queen-size bed. I'm going to paint, redo your bathroom, and add a steam shower. Maybe a nice desk in the corner. Your grandmother Martin might stay over."

I suspect the truth is Mom's going to move in here. A nice, quiet, non-divorce separate living arrangement she's been waiting for since around the time I was in middle school. She'll blame Dad's snoring. He'll spend more time at Rolling Green, she'll start hosting girls' weekends to Vegas, and they'll never even see each other except passing the halls.

I also suspect this is how most marriages work. It doesn't really bother me. It's not like they fight.

"Yeah, I'll get on it," I say, still snuggled in bed, sighing contentedly.

"Now, mister," she says as she walks down the hall. "You've got a lot to do."

This is the way I'd thought I'd feel after Oneida's. Maybe it's just a delayed reaction, but this morning I feel…

OK, this sounds fricking stupid, but I actually feel good, like *smiling-for-no-reason* good, *jump-out-of-bed-and-start-the-day* good. I didn't realize how depressed I'd been about not getting laid. Or… OK, if I said this out loud, I'd expect someone to punch me, but, for the first time in a long time, I feel happy.

I did it. I found someone willing to touch me, willing to let me touch them. Someone who laughs when I say stuff instead of getting offended.

I peek out the top of my covers. Mom's gone, but of course she's left the door open so I don't go back to sleep.

Sleep is not on my mind. But I do wish that door was closed.

I can't wait to see him again. I grab my phone, promising myself I'll pack this morning and go see Lucas this afternoon.

First, I realize it's already almost noon. No wonder I'm starving.

Second, I see I texted him three times last night and he hasn't responded once.

That happiness? It wilts.

Maybe he thought I was insulting him with that two hundred bucks.

Maybe I'm nothing more than a needy john to him, a job.

I feel myself spiraling into doubt. I need to talk to him. If I see his face, I know I can make him laugh again, and then this will be OK.

I think about the knee flirting distance lesson from last night. I probably shouldn't call if he hasn't responded to a text. How many times can you text someone before it gets uncomfortable?

I think about texting this question to Lucas as a joke.

I shake it off, decide to stay calm.

Lucas likes me. I know. And that's because I have tons of experience with people *not* liking me, and Lucas doesn't act like that.

All the same, I decide I'm going to clean out my stuff, say goodbye to my childhood bedroom, and wait for Lucas to answer my texts. And if he doesn't answer by say... four? I'll take a break and swing by Rolling Green, try and scope out if he's pissed at me.

16
———

Lucas

I call my boss Ron from the hospital's parking lot, apologize that I'm going to be late for my job at Rolling Green.

"Don't sweat it," Ron says when he hears I'm with Kit. Kit scowls though.

"I hate being an excuse," she mutters.

"Quit feeling sorry for yourself," I tease her as I hang up with Ron.

She shoves me, snapping out of her self-pity. "At least maybe now you'll stop flirting with all my doctors," she sasses, trying to get the upper hand because she knows about Theo.

"Oh, I'll still be flirting." I reverse the car and pull out of the parking.

"Well I get Cheadle," she says like he's a trading card instead of the Phlebotomist.

The whole way home, we argue who gets which hot medical staff. I let her have Cheadle.

I drop Kit off, reminding her to do her summer home-school work before Mom gets back so we can go out to Music at the Park this evening. Kit's got extra school work to make up for the time she can't get it done because of medical issues. Once again, Kit scowls at me, but who *doesn't* scowl about homework?

I break a few speed limits getting to work.

Ron's taken care of opening, and I apologize to him again as I rush in. He brushes me off, telling me it's no big deal. It's a hard line to walk— being kind to my family because of Kit or treating us with pity. Ron walks it well.

He's done all the opening work and a waiter Ron's stolen from the clubhouse makes sure I've got the Snack Shack covered before jogging back to the main building. Now all I've got to do is grab a tablet and start taking orders.

As I tie on my apron, Theo marches up to the pool.

God, he is handsome.

"What's up?" I fall into my routine here at the pool, using my employee-speak as I straighten my apron.

"You didn't text me back," he says.

"Oh. Sorry, man. My... never mind." I don't want to tell him about Kit. Not like this— presenting her as an excuse. It's her private life, her body, and it feels wrong to talk about her to other people without Kit's permission.

This is exactly why I can't have a boyfriend: I'm late taking Kit to her appointment, then late to work. I forgot to answer Theo's texts and he's mad. I'm on my back foot. All the questions I have about last night flood through me. The two hundred dollars in my pocket. And Theo doesn't even know why I need it, even if I don't want to take it.

I run a hand through my hair. Did I even brush it this morning? I've been going full speed since I woke up, without a minute to think of anything except what's right in front of me.

Theo's smile is completely gone when I look up.

"Look, whatever I did wrong, I'm sorry," he says.

"What?" I laugh, embarrassed.

"I thought maybe I didn't pay you enough, or you were mad because I left—"

I give him a warning look to lower his voice. "It's fine. We should figure out what we're doing here, Theo, but I'm not mad. I just had to take care of some things. My life is really full right now, and I don't know—"

I see him see where I'm going with this. Theo's been rejected enough times, I realize, to have heard this speech before.

"Because I like you," he interrupts in a loud, clear voice.

It shocks me silent. Theo's a bro and he's chased after girls for as long as I can remember. To be honest, I thought he'd have at minimum, a *smidge* of internalized homophobia going on. But here he is, announcing he likes me for everyone at Rolling Green who cared to overhear.

Unlike me, Theo does not look to see who might be around.

"Crap. I'm screwing this up," Theo mutters. He scuffs his sneaker across the concrete.

"No," I start to reach for his hand, think better of it.

A dozen or so country club members are lounging at the pool, some of them watching with not-so-discreet interest. I flinch, hating the situation. After all, I'm 'Lucky' to a few of them, and seeing me mix it up with a romantic interest doesn't help business. Everyone wants to be the only one.

In a quieter voice, I say, "No. You're not screwing this up at all."

I swallow hard. Thinking about clients has made me remember the video of me, O, and Theo. Shit. When he sees it, he's going to realize whatever is between us now, initially I took money to set him up and screw him over.

Theo's going to hate me when that tape comes out. And he'll be right.

"Good." Theo grins, relieved. "Because I want to spend every day with you until I have to go to school. And I want to... I want you to come visit me, and I'm going to come home like every weekend. I want to see as much of you as I can."

My heart. Holy shit, my heart feels like it's going to explode, caught between wanting and knowing I'm going to lose.

Who would've thought Theo had this in him?

I duck my head and clear my throat. "Look. Last night was great. Really great." I frown, unsure what to say about the money he left me. I want to give it back. But I also know there's a stack of bills waiting to be paid. "Let's talk after work, OK?"

Ah, here's the Old Theo I'm used to. His head snaps back, look on his face like he's vaguely insulted to be in my presence. He runs a hand through his hair.

"Yeah, OK," he nods, finally looks around as if he's just become aware of the loungers.

"I mean it," I say.

"Sure, what time do you get off?" he asks.

Shit. "Oh wait. I have this thing I promised Kit."

"Yeah. OK. I'll see you around."

"Theo, wait." I try to say his name with as much force as I can without letting everyone at the pool know I'm falling for this guy.

Already out of the corner of my eye, one of my regulars appears quite pissy I haven't taken her order. After all, I work here. I'm currently wasting time talking to someone who is neither making a pool order nor requesting my help in any Rolling Green employee-related way.

Ron goes to take her order. Crap.

"Look, I want to see you," I say as Theo retreats. "Every chance I can. And coming to see you at school sounds great."

I blush at *coming*, but Theo's still clearly trying to decipher what I mean with all my mixed signals.

A cart of golfers rolls in, parks near the putting green, and the four white-gloved old dudes go for the Snack Shak, probably to get a few drinks and cool off. One of the men breaks off from the foursome and it doesn't take half a second to recognize Theo's dad.

"Theo!" Mr. Benedict calls, all showroom floor Dad style, definitely putting on the act of being a happy family man in front of the other golfers in his group.

When he spots me, the smile stays, the eyes go cold.

"Hey Dad," Theo says.

"Mr. Benedict." I nod.

He turns his full attention to Theo and talks at length about his son's plans for cleaning out his bedroom to convert it to a guest room. The moment I step back to excuse myself, Mr. Benedict says, "Ah, gin and tonic, if you don't mind."

I swallow my irritation. Mr. Benedict knows me. He knows my family because his hospital treats Kit. My mother got dressed in her Sunday best and stood in front of his board making pleas for charity. What I'm trying to say is he knows my name. But he still chooses to treat me as a faceless servant, not bothering to speak to me except for his G&T order.

"Right away, sir," I say, maybe a touch overly ass-kissy, because Mr. Benedict cuts me a glance like, *watch it.*

When I come back with the drink, Theo's gone.

Mr. Benedict takes the Gin & Tonic, signs with a line on the tab, winks, and says, "Thanks, Lucky," before walking away.

* * *

IT EATS AT ME THE REST OF THE SHIFT. I KNOW THEO'S disappointed, and finally I text him.

Me: *I want to see you too.*

Me: *Give me a minute to handle something first.*

I study the phone, trying to see it from Theo's perspective. The money he left me. The texts I didn't answer. The way I handled things at the pool. From the outside, Theo seems like he has everything— looks, money, confidence. I bet a dozen people have broken his heart not realizing that underneath those things, he's unsure and awkward and trying really hard to make a connection.

None of this helps me with my larger problem of the tape.

It's seven and the sun is low in the sky, giving everything a golden glow with violet shadows. It's getting darker earlier now. Summer is almost over.

But the evening air is warm, and the pool waves make splashing sounds as some older fellows come out from the clubhouse and do a few sedate laps now that the kids are gone.

I start my clean-up routine, prepping to lock up the Snack Shack, thinking about Theo, and about being late for Kit's appointment. I go back and forth a hundred times, telling myself I can't juggle a relationship right now. Theo can be my secret, the promise of a romance in the distance, something to keep me going.

But then I think best case scenario, Kit's *always* going to need help. I can't really wish for anything outcome other than that. And it's fine. I am handling it. This is the first time I've screwed things up in a long time.

Foot-in-his-mouth Theo. Handsome, arrogant, asshole Theo. Who stood in front of everyone who might be listening at Rolling Green and said he liked me. Not even hesitating before he said it.

I wipe the sweat off my brown. I'm working at an insane pace to get out of here, hurriedly wiping down the surfaces in the Snack Shak, running the mop across the floor, prepping all the items so I can pull the metal shields over the valuables.

I want to see him. One missed appointment doesn't mean I can't learn to find room for Theo in my life.

But there's one thing I've got to clear up first.

I text Oneida.

Me: *You have a minute for me?*

She answers right away

The Fab O: *Are you at the club*

Me: *Yeah, you?*

The Fab O: *I'm taking dinner in the clubhouse.*

Me: *I'll be there in fifteen.*

I finish securing the Snack Shack and drag the 'pool closed' sign out to the front of the pool's steps. The rich people of Rolling Green do not care for signs that change their plans, and they'll take a dip if they want. Ron says it's for insurance if their drunk asses drown while there's no lifeguard on duty.

A group of men wearing the club's dress code of 'smart casual' come out of the main building to light up cigars. The embers glow across the lawn.

I make note of them merely because after working for Oneida I've become aware of older husbands. Most of them look right through me, but one or two seem to watch me with secret knowledge. So far, though, they don't seem angry. Or at least, not any more or less angry and irritable than usual, which baffles me. They have so much money! They are living lives of luxury! What could possibly make them so disgruntled with everything that catches their eye?

A few of them nod speculatively at me, as if we share the secret knowledge of how their wives spend time with me.

One of the most interesting things about working for Oneida is discovering that while everyone at Rolling Green touts monogamy, matrimony, and going to church every Sunday, behind closed doors, these rich people's relationships aren't limited to the narrowly defined romances I grew up with in movies and TV. Half of them don't even care what their partners do.

I give a respectful nod as I pass them, the smell of their cigars pungent in the evening air. Then it's inside the clubhouse, where I'm woefully underdressed, even for staff.

Oneida's sitting with a group of similar-aged women at a round booth near the back. It's all wine glasses, salads, and knowing laughter from the table. She beckons me with a crooked finger.

"Hello, ladies." I smile at the circle of tipsy, knowing, hungry faces. "Oneida, I'm sorry, do you have a moment?"

I practically bow in deference. Oneida likes her prestige. It also works out for me as a little advertisement. I feel Oneida's companions studying me.

"Excuse me." Oneida apologizes with a cat-with-the-cream smile and wiggles out of the booth.

She is in a chocolate brown dress that flows over her curves. The material is sparkly at one angle and matte from the other, eye-catching without seeming desperate for attention. She is also working tonight, and at least three guys at the gleaming bar at the far end of the club-house pretend not to watch her move. I get that I increase her sex appeal. Everyone wants to know what the deal is with us, if we're lovers, and if so, how good she must be in bed to keep a young guy like me wrapped around her finger.

Maybe this is why she is so willing to talk to me in the middle of her dinner.

"What can I do for you?" Oneida practically purrs.

I motion for her to take a few more steps into the hall-way. This is still not entirely private, but it's the best I can do.

I lean into her, practically nuzzling my face into her neck, which I feel her arch gracefully. "The tape. Theo's?"

"Mmmm?"

"Can I talk you out of sending it?"

She pulls back, confused.

I say, "I think it's a mistake. If Theo's dad finds out, he's not going to like—"

"Benedict knows?" She looks nervous.

"I don't know," I say honestly, and my excitement surges that this is going to work. If that tape doesn't go out, I am free and clear with Theo. "But what's he going to say if he finds out you helped blackmail his kid?"

Oneida purses her lips, biting the bottom one in a way she probably doesn't even realize is sexy. Some people just have a gift. It distracts me for a moment, and so I don't quite pick up how she's not really scared so much as...

"I just think it's a good idea to trash it," I say confidently.

A slow smile crosses her face, and it hits me she's not worried at all. She's excited. Oneida wants Theo's dad to know what she did. Something is going on with them I

hadn't counted on. She sighs, a waft of her perfume, intox-
icating.

And then she says the worst thing: "Sorry, Lucky. I already sent it out." I feel my face go cold. She adds, "*Days ago.*"

17

When the valet arrives with my car, I stalk from the steps of Rolling Green, get in, and slam the door.

My car at least has headroom, unlike Lucas' stupid freaking shitmobile. I can't believe he's blowing me off. I can't believe I was actually happy about Lucas this time yesterday.

Although it's true I'm not so great at flirting, or catching signals from girls, one thing I have plenty of experience with: when someone's embarrassed to be seen with me. I felt that way today. At Rolling Green, where I'm a member and he is staff, Lucas was embarrassed to be seen with me.

I punch the wheel and the horn gives a short squeaky bleat, sounding as impotent as I feel. I lay on it with my palm and make it blare. The valets look at me like I'm an asshole.

Of course. What Theo did to me he does for a living. Shame burns my guts until it physically hurts. I am the hugest stereotype of cringey, desperate behavior. I have fallen for a guy just working his side hustle.

As I gun the engine and speed down the slow, speed-bump-lined, curving exit of Rolling Green, desperate to escape my humiliation, I see Hailey walking up the road for her shift at the Snack Shack. Hailey, another rejection. Hailey, who would rather be Jack's sidepiece than give me the time of day.

I screech to a stop and she jumps up on the curb, stumbling a little into the lush green lawn. Before I even roll down the window, she looks nervous. No surprise there—we've never been on great terms.

"Hey, Hails."

"Theo," she sniffs.

"Where's Jack these days?" I haven't exactly hung out with Jack since the night of the fair. Another relationship I messed up being stupid.

"Why don't you call him and find out?" she says with fake sweetness as she continues walking toward the club. I throw the car in reverse to move with her.

Man, she really hates me, I realize. Is this how I want to live my life, with everyone around barely tolerating me?

"Hey, Hails. Blow off work and come hang out with me. We'll go get ice cream or something," I say.

I start to make a joke about licking stuff and how Ella and Jack both might like that, but since I am barely two seconds out of my grief about how nobody likes me, I decide not to joke. People don't seem to like it.

She laughs. "Some of us have to work. Paying your *black-mailer* to visit a *hooker* isn't cheap."

"Ah come on..." I start to say how it wasn't that much money, how Hailey works all the time.

Hailey scowls at me, and in turning her face my way to do it, I see she's got bluish shadows under her eyes. She looks a little scrawny actually. I can't imagine where her money's going since community college is free, but it makes me wonder if I misjudged her situation.

"Yeah, well, I had a great time," I say instead.

"Yeah, I know." She scoffs.

"And I'd like to thank you for being so cool about everything." I think of how Lucas said he's busy tonight, and how I'm friendless and alone. "Can I take you out to dinner?"

Hailey stops walking and gives me a sincerely pissed-off sneer. "No thanks."

Am I not making an effort?

"What, you got plans with your boyfriend? Or your girlfriend? Both?" I regret saying it as soon as it's out of my mouth, so I add, "I'm jealous as frick."

"Maybe Jack's too much of your friend to tell you, but we don't care if everyone knows about us so your little blackmail scheme isn't worth shit."

"My trip to Oneida's proves it's been worth *something*," I counter.

"Yeah, how's it feel that you have to pay people to pretend they want you?" she's marching fast up the slight hill. My car whines in reverse to keep up.

Her comment stings. She is sweaty and red-faced, and it gets through that she is really angry with me.

"Yeah, well what's it like for your boyfriend *and* girlfriend to pay not to be seen with you?"

Something about that really gets under her skin, although I don't know why— this town would flip its shit if Ella Stewart was in a threesome on video. Hailey's got to know that's how this town works.

"Surprise, asshole." She pulls up her phone, face a mix of fury and victory. "Jack didn't want to use this because he is your friend. But I've got a copy too. So take a close look at how you are never, ever going to bother us again. Or else this goes out and everyone to everyone in town."

On her phone is a video of Oneida's living room. Oneida's going down on me, head bobbing in my lap. On the couch next to me, the back of Lucas' head as we kiss. The back of Oneida's body is blurred out, as is all of Lucas's body except his forearm. It appears I'm being banged by two blobs.

Ha, banged by two blobs is the name of my sex tape. The thought comes out of left field.

The room behind us is strangely absent of any personality, although that wasn't true in real life. It's the camera angle, positioned to make the place as anonymous as possible. It looks like the suite section in a business class hotel room.

My face isn't blurred though, at least not until Lucas kisses me. I am open-mouthed, eyes closed, obviously enjoying myself as I lose my blow job virginity on camera. Hailey lets it roll until I cum, shuddering.

I look at Hailey. Her eyes glisten with tears, full of fury and contempt and triumph.

"Will you send me a copy of that?" I ask.

18

Lucas

I'm pacing the Snack Shack when Hailey comes in.

"Hey, you OK?" She gives me a weird look and I realize I never pace.

"Right back at you," I answer. Her face is blotchy and it looks like she's been crying.

"Yeah." She nods, smiling until tears leak from the corners of her eyes, clearly not OK. Or at least, only recently OK.

I pluck a paper napkin from the dispenser and give it to her. She blows her nose with a honk, wads the napkin, and makes a basket from four feet away. I hand her another. This time she delicately blots under her eyes, trying to preserve make-up or sunscreen, or whatever makes women do that gesture.

"Ugh. Theo." She shakes her head and sighs.

I go perfectly still, having somehow forgotten how to act casual. "Oh? What'd he do?"

"Nothing worth ruining the day over," Hailey says. "I'll be right back."

She flounces off to the employee dressing room. I want to grab her and demand the whole story. But doing that would probably make Hailey have some questions of her own.

When she returns, her face is fresh again and she's tying her apron while scanning the pool area for customers.

"Was this that blackmail thing?" This is the clever line I've put together during her absence.

She looks at me like she's forgotten what we were talking about. Or forgotten that she told me about the blackmail. Or that I know it's got something to do with Theo. She slides through all those expressions and then shrugs, nonchalant.

"It's taken care of," she says.

"Oh? How?"

"Jack took care of it. Or he was going to, but..."

My heart makes lodging in my throat. Good old soft-hearted Jack. He hasn't shown Theo the tape. This makes complete sense. Those guys have been best friends forever. Jack probably knows that if Theo sees that video of me, Theo, and Oneida, Theo will go scorched earth.

"... so I took care of it," Hailey says.

"Excuse me, what?"

She pops out of the Snack Shack to take an order, leaving me to wonder exactly what Hailey took care of.

When Hailey comes back in, she's got a flurry of questions about the Pops and who is going, and whether I've seen Ella and I can't find a way to steer the conversation back to what Hailey said.

I sweat a little, trying to keep my charming Lucky face on as I go out to help the pool loungers.

Jack and Theo have been best friends forever, is the mantra going through my head. *If Theo wouldn't forgive Jack, how will he ever forgive me?*

* * *

Theo

I pound on Jack's door.

"I know you're there," I say in a loud voice. "Your car's here."

Jack's mom opens the door. "Theo!" she scolds.

"Oh! Sorry. Is Jack here?"

She narrows her eyes at me. "From what I heard through the door—"

"Sorry about that," I say.

"—you've used your infinite powers of deduction to figure it out."

I hang my head. Being tall, this only gives her a better view of my embarrassed face.

"What's going on with you two?" she demands.

"Nothing!"

She gives me the look. The one that says she smells bullshit. "Are you here to start trouble?"

"No!"

She gives me a skeptical up and down. I think distractedly that if I *was* here to start trouble, I'd flirt with her. My time with Oneida has opened my eyes to the hotness quotient of older ladies. How they knew things.

"Ma, it's OK, I got this." Jack comes to the door, looking like he just woke up.

He's holding his phone, probably glancing at my texts that I'm coming over. Or Hailey's texts about what she did.

Jack's mom gives me another long scowl and I realize for the millionth time that something about me makes people not entirely trust me. I must have the guy equivalent of resting bitch face. I make an effort to smile.

"Be nice," she orders, poking my chest with her index finger before leaving us.

"You wanna..." Jack gestures to his room. He knows why I'm here, that we need privacy to work this out.

It's been weeks since I've been over to his house. All the familiar details come rushing back making me miss Jack more now that I'm here. My family's always had money and nice things. We've paid for Jack to go on vacation to Hawaii with us twice, and he's tagged along skiing a couple of times on our dime too. That's what I donate to the friendship.

Jack, on the other hand... OK, this is super cheesy, but his family actually gets along. His mom and stepdad like each other. When I'd sleep over, they'd stay up in the living room, watching movies together. Or sometimes after dinner, we'd all play cards. When we first started being friends, I thought it was fake. The way my parents act when they go to parties together. But it isn't. Jack is just a lucky bastard who has the rare family that likes each other. I come over and watch it, like a TV show.

Now jack leads me past the dining room and the kitchen, down a cramped hallway to his room. He hasn't opened his windows so it's dark and dank in here, smelling like a gym bag.

"Bro, air it out." I go to the window and throw it open.

Jack closes his door, shoves his hands in his pockets, and waits to hear why I'm here.

We haven't really hung out since the night of the fair. I'd thought the video I'd taken was funny as hell, and I'd assumed Jack was making a show of being mad. I mean, who the frick would be embarrassed to be living every dude's dream, right?! But he *was* pissed.

And then *I* got mad at *him*—my best friend had this whole life he was keeping secret from me, screwing the girl he knew I liked, and being all butt hurt about me finding out about it.

I figured he'd pay for Oneida and we'd be even, it'd be cool. We'd go back to how it was. Which isn't a stupid plan — my dad gets out of all his mistakes by buying stuff for the people he's offended. Jewelry for Mom, dinners out with his buddies.

And.... OK, if I'm going to be really honest, I don't know how to say goodbye to Jack.

We've been friends for a long time, constant buddies for parties and sports. I'm going to State. Last I heard, Jack was either going to school with Ella, or maybe going to Community College, but either way, we won't see each other next year. It's sad and I don't know how to handle that.

"Hailey told me," Jack says.

"I'm gonna miss you," I blurt out at the same time.

We both say, "What?" at the same time.

I grin. Jack frowns.

I say, "Oh, yeah. Hailey showed me the video of me getting blown at Oneida's."

Jack looks miserable, shoves his hands deeper into his pockets. "Yeah well. She shouldn't have done that." He trails off. Clears his throat. "I'm sorry, man. Ella talked to me about it. It was uncool of us to do that."

I laugh, too loud and practically braying like a jackass. Sometimes I hear myself, but by then it's too late. "Nah, man. It's frickin' funny."

"What?" Jack looks at me like he doesn't quite trust me not to throw a punch. I wonder if maybe that's why he put his hands in his pockets like that— to stop himself from hitting back if I started up.

I nod, then shake my head. "Yeah, no. I mean, it's kind of perfect. I thought I was funny as hell taking that video of you guys." Jack flushes as I say that, so I hurry on. "But then it kind of got away from me."

"What do you mean? Who has it?" he interrupts angrily.

"Oh. No! The *video* didn't get away from me. I'm the only one who's seen it. What happened was *you* didn't think it was funny, but I thought it was a slug-bug."

Slug-bug was this game we used to play on car rides. If one of us saw a VW Bug first, we'd call 'slug-bug' and hit the other guy. You didn't *apologize* for that. It was a *game*. You just bided your time until the next slug-bug, and then you waled the living frick out of your best friend, screaming slug-bug so he knew the rules.

Jack looks at me like my nuts are hanging out of the top of my shorts.

I roll my eyes in exasperation. "I tried to even it out, is all."

"You mean blackmail us."

"So it would be even!" I defend myself. How can Jack think I'm that huge of an asshole? "I can't just delete it and pretend that shit didn't happen."

"That's exactly what a friend would've done!" Jack's hands come out of his pockets. Uh-oh.

I shake my head again. "You don't delete things that happen, you bond over that shit. Like when Kevin shit his pants on the bus home from All-State—"

Jack laughs all of the sudden, *like, yeah I remember*. Because of course. Everyone remembers. "And everyone called him 'All Shit' after that."

"The guy shit his pants! We're gonna pretend like we didn't notice? How does that help? Giving him a nickname, laughing about it? That's what being friends is about."

"That's what being a bully is all about." Jack's laughter is gone like it never happened.

"I can't believe you..." *thought that.* But I have this problem a lot. People always think my default is cruelty. I scowl. Even Jack, who's known me for years.

It hits me that if Jack's known me for years, and he thinks I'm a bully, maybe I am a bully.

Holy shit. I hang my head.

Jack grunts. "You're saying you blackmailed us because we're friends?"

"Yeah, OK, maybe I took it too far. But come on. I've been trying since freshman year to get laid and you guys are doing that and... and you left me out."

An irritable laugh. "Did you want an invite?"

"Frick no," I laugh. Which is kind of a lie. "Yeah maybe, I guess? I wanted to have fun this summer, and you were all wrapped up in them. And you knew I liked Hailey!"

"Theo, there is no way I'm apologizing for not inviting you to share my girlfriends."

"Oh man, do you hear yourself?" I scoff, pacing. I can't pace much because his room is pretty small.

"Fine." I stop. "But you know what? You did the same thing to me that I did to you."

"And it was a mistake. I said so. Theo, I wasn't going to ever show you that video—"

"Plus, you've got to admit I have had a shitty dating streak, and it had something to do with you and Hailey lying to me about Hailey even being remotely interested in dating me."

Slowly Jack nods.

"So maybe I took it too far. But just cut me out..." All of the sudden, and totally unexpectedly, I choke up. I blink, looking away, and go mess with Jack's window so I don't have to face him.

I thought I'd pushed him away and I'd lost my best

friend, I realize. Maybe that's why I'd thrown myself so hard and fast into this thing with Lucas.

I clear my throat. "That's why the video you took from Oneida's is so great," I say.

"I'm... not following?"

I turn back, give him my best smile. "You have a tape, I have a tape. We're even."

Jack makes a weird face as he thinks through it. "Yeah, I guess."

I shrug. "Think it through, dude. You know I'm never gonna share that video. Or if I do, you've got one to share too. It's like nuclear cold war or whatever. Peace through superior firepower."

"So you'll destroy yours and I'll destroy ours?"

"Hell no." I laugh. "That shit is funny. I'm definitely keeping a copy."

Jack does punch me then, but in the bicep, only hard enough for the muscle there to lose feeling. "Frick, man! Ow!"

19

———

LUCAS

Music in the Park is sponsored by the county, which means it's free. Or at least already paid for by taxes. It starts around 7 and goes until 9:30, so lots of people show up early and have picnic dinners on the grass. Food trucks show up. When the music starts, people bust out the wine and joints and dance. Little kids swing and run around the playground nearby. It's a vibe.

Sometimes I catch the crowd from Rolling Green here, with their high-end grass-woven picnic baskets and folding chairs, especially in the height of summer when things get boring and the rich start trolling for cheap thrills. But for the most part, the Rolling Green crowd seems to stay away from events that let everyone in. Which means I can relax and enjoy myself.

Kit loves Music in the Park. For one thing, the kids from her school hang out there, grouping up and sneaking off to the far end of the park to do kid stuff. She doesn't need an invite, just runs off with them. I love those freaking kids.

Mom puts her baseball hat down low over her eyes and

half-sleeps, listening to the music. Or she'll get energized when it's an oldies cover band. She'll start bets with the other picnickers on who can name the tune first. They scream out titles I've never heard before and then cackle when they are the first to call it correctly.

Not too many people my age come to Music in the Park. We're too old to sneak off to the baseball diamond to play truth or dare, too young to have babies and picnic blankets. Still, it's nice enough to feel the breeze and listen to music. Usually.

Tonight, all I can think of is Theo.

"What's up?" Mom asks from underneath her baseball cap.

I rub my eye. "Nothing, just tired."

"Don't lie to your mother," she says.

But she does it in this easy way like she knows I'm keeping stuff from her but she's not going to pry. She's just going to let me know I am not successful in my attempts to hide things from her.

I laugh and we listen to music a little bit more. In the distance, Kit is standing in a group with five or six kids. One of them does a handstand.

Mom sits up. "Your friends are going to college soon."

"Yep," I agree.

Now it's her turn to sigh. I know she wants to tell me I should apply to go somewhere next year, but we both know I can't. I can do it little by little, one class at a time.

I inhale deeply, hoping for a second-hand high from the joint someone's lit in the near distance. Mom gives me a smirk. I catch Hailey and Jack showing up, holding hands. They don't sit, but wander around the edge of the park, strolling, talking. They make a cute couple. They also look like they are sneaking off to do something horny. Or maybe that's just their chemistry.

"Tell me something good," Mom says instead.

"I met someone," I say.

She sits up. "What?!" My mom squeals like a teenager. "Who? Tell me everything."

I shrug, my face getting hot.

"Oh no!" she laughs delightedly pinching my cheek. "Look at that! You are *in love!*"

"No. It's not like that." I shrug, checking Kit in the distance. Her group of friends are passing around something and I squint to make sure it's not a roach. After a moment, I'm satisfied. From this distance, it appears to be something from the food carts. Probably candy. There's this dude who makes jawbreakers. Pure sugar, but layered with wild colors. Kids suck on them and stick their tongues out at each other. They're pretty popular. Sure enough, I see a bluish-looking tongue being stuck out and laughter mimed between the strains of music.

"What's it like then?" Mom asks in a subdued tone, which makes me realize I'm frowning.

"I messed it up."

She matches my frown. We listen to music for a while.

"But you like her?"

I nod, letting the gender thing slide. I don't think she'd care, but she might start taking my fawning doctor worship a little more seriously if she knew.

"Well, then, unmess it up," she says.

I laugh. "How am I going to do that?"

She shrugs. "You're the Brainiac, you'll figure it out."

"It doesn't matter. School's going to start, and they'll be gone."

She catches the 'they', and smiles like she does when she learns a new thing about me.

"Well, perfect then. You can practice unmessing something up, and if you totally cake it, your mystery romantic interest will go off to school and it's like it never happened. If you manage to woo them back, you get to wipe that lovesick look off your face."

I lean back. "Maybe it'll hurt more if I do win them back and they leave."

She tilts the hat back over her eyes. "Your mama didn't raise no cowards."

I rub my face, check my phone. No calls from Theo.

"I can't really unmess it up," I say finally. "I did something... mean to them."

"Lucas!" Mom slaps me lightly on the leg, scolding. "What did you do?"

"It's complicated," I say.

"Well then. Try apologizing. If you're sorry. But don't if you're not. It's not nice to say things just to get someone to like you. You have to be true."

I pluck single blades of grass. "Yes ma'am."

"What do you like about them?" she asks.

I open my mouth to answer, my eye flickering over to Kit.

She's on the ground, on her hands and knees. Her face is the wrong color. The girl next to her screams.

I am on my feet. I am running. But as other people turn to look, they move in their seats. Kit's back is humped and convulsing like she's throwing up. But no puke. Music in the Parkers get up, start moving toward her or talking to each other, getting in my way.

I dodge between them, but I'm so far away, and soon they stand, and I can't see Kit. Shouts. Something bad's happening.

I run to the field where the group of kids stand. They all stare at Kit's shuddering form. Time slows down and I catch how one of them has tears running down his face even as he refuses to move, to even blink.

"Kit?" I reach her. My little sister's eyes bulge, her color bad, no sound at all coming from her.

"Move!" A familiar voice demands.

I look up. The crowd doesn't exactly part so much as get shoved aside.

"Help!" I yell. "Someone call 911!"

Kit's conscious, but it is a horrible kind of alertness. She's not breathing.

I open her mouth and swish my finger across her tongue. She bites me, thrashing, but with the very tip of my finger pad, I feel something rough, solid.

"She's choking!" I shout.

And then that familiar voice— Hailey— is there.

"Move." She likewise shoves me out of the way as she did with the rubberneckers surrounding us. I fall on my ass.

Hailey, a certified lifeguard, starts the first aid check.

"It's in her throat!" I yell.

A kid sobs and runs away. I barely notice.

Hailey does the Heimlich maneuver on Kit. She straddles my little sister's legs and puts the heel of her hand in the space between Kit's belly button and the bottom of her ribcage. Then she shoves, hard.

Someone screams, "You'll break her ribs!"

Hailey ignores the critique. What good will perfect ribs do Kit if she chokes to death?

Kit writhes in an attempt to hork up the thing blocking her throat, eerily silent.

Hailey shoves again, grunting with the effort. The hiss of air. Something pink lolls along Kit's lip and she turns her head, coughing and sputtering. It falls out. A jawbreaker the size of a marble, pink on one side, green peeking through on the other.

Hailey falls to the side and I crawl over to Kit, who is gasping wildly, coughing. I am sobbing.

"You saved her," someone says, almost conversationally.

But it picks up, and lots of people start saying it too. Then they start clapping for Hailey, cheering her. An ambulance arrives, lights blaring at the side of the park.

EMTs show up and take Kit to the ambulance on a stretcher. I already know an ambulance ride costs $1700, but this is what it's like to deal with health insurance. I have a fleeting, sour sense of satisfaction that I wasn't able to pay Oneida back my part of the 3K to get her to erase Theo's video. I'm not sorry.

My mother meets us as the EMTs get across the lawn. She throws her arms around Kit, and when the EMTs pull her back, she throws her arms around me. It's a big spectacle, but thank goodness Hailey stays put and the crowd gathers around her, congratulating her, asking her where she learned to save a life.

Together, Mom and I follow as they take Kit. Mom's not crying. She's cried for Kit too many times to go waterworks for something like this that is already looking better.

"It's going to be OK," I mutter over and over like a prayer as I get into the ambulance with my little sister.

"I'm fine," she says, froggy voiced and still coughing. "Let me go home, I'm fine."

"You might have damage to your esophagus," one of the EMTs chides her.

I nod. She should get checked out.

Mom tugs at my hand. "I'll ride with her," she says.

I nod, yeah of course. Moms go with their children.

"I'll take the car home," I say. And then, so Kit can hear, "That was so lucky. Kit, for a kid with a lot of bad luck, you sure have a ton of good luck."

They have an oxygen mask over her so she just gives me a thumbs up. I think about what oxygen in the ambulance costs. I get out.

"She *is* lucky," Mom says, getting into the spare seat in the back of the ambulance. "You are too." And then she says, "Go unmistake your situation."

I nod like I'm not going to. Mom reaches out and pinches my arm. "Ouch!"

She leans in, good and mad, and says in a quiet hiss, "Life's too short, Lucas. Do it."

"But Kit..."

"I got her. I'll call when we need a ride home."

I see this close that I was mistaken. She is not crying like she does when something really bad happens, but her eyes are shiny and bloodshot.

It really hits me then that Kit could've died. If not for Hailey, or even with Hailey. Mom's right. Life is short. Too short.

This time, I nod for real, squeeze the keys in my pocket.

Satisfied, Mom leans back and the EMT shows her how to buckle up, as though this is Mom's first time in an ambulance.

The doors close, and they are gone.

I turn to thank Hailey, and she's still surrounded by onlookers. Some guy with a real camera is taking her picture. I push through all of them and throw my arms around her.

"Thank you, Hailey. Thank you. Thank you," I say real loud. My words are muffled by the cheering crowd. When I let go, the guy with the camera asks for Hailey's name, then mine, then Kit's. I don't tell him Kit's, because that's Kit's business, not anyone else's. He tells me he's a local reporter who came to cover Music in the Park and he's going to make a story of the rescue.

I tell him that's great. Hailey blushes and smiles and shakes hands.

"You're gonna be famous," I tease her as I say goodbye. She absolutely beams.

I run to the car and text Theo.

Me: *Where are you*

My heart beats too slow and then too fast. The bubbles come right away.

Theo: *Jack's*

He knows. I'm too late to even confess ahead of the truth and spin it in a light most favorable to Theo forgiving me.

Fuck. I about throw my phone to the ground, despite the fact I can't afford to replace it, when it buzzes in my hand.

Theo: *Wanna come over?*

My heart. I don't even know what I'm feeling it's beating so hard.

20

––––––

LUCAS

What am I doing? Probably voluntarily arriving to my own beat down. Wasting gas to get there. The fuck is wrong with me?

My phone buzzes and I check it, in case it's about Kit. But it's Oneida asking me to check in. Probably scheduling a date for me. I ignore it, even though it's money at the other end of that text, which theoretically should be much more appealing than my current destination.

I know generally where Jack lives— it's not like we're best friends or anything, but we did go to high school together, and living in a town this size, you get a sense of where people are located. This is an older neighborhood where there are maybe four different floor plans, but with time everything's both a little run down in places and then kind of funky with additions and garage conversions so that none of the houses really look identical anymore. More like cousins.

Theo sends me the address anyway, and I pull up in front of Jack's house. The two of them are out on the porch, drinking from beer bottles. They are so easy with each other. Theo's never mean to Jack that I can tell, and this flare of jealousy burns brighter than my bewildered sense of *what-the-fuck-are-you-doing-Lucas?*

I kill the engine and stare through the windshield at them for a minute, waiting to see if they're gonna come after me with fists swinging.

Theo gets up. I think to myself about who I want to be, and whether the answer is:

a coward who flees the scene

or

a guy who can't work for a few weeks because the ladies don't like a guy with a smashed face and bruised ribs.

Our eyes meet. Or I think they do at least. It's dark and Theo's features are shadowed by the house lights behind him. He's coming across the grass.

I get out, approaching with some trepidation. Inside, I'm wondering how messed up life is that I should be going the other direction, but I want him. I need to tell him I'm sorry to his face. And I desperately want him to...

"Theo, I'm sorry," I say when we are a few feet apart. I hang my head. It was a really shitty thing to do.

"What for?" he says, taking a last swig off his beer and tossing the bottle into the grass. He is going to make me say everything I did before he beats the shit out of me.

"For the video thing at O's. I didn't know you then like I know...." I shake my head. "But I did know about it when it was happening. That was wrong. I'm sorry."

Distantly, it clicks in my head how weird it is that Jack isn't black and blue. Neither is Theo.

"... Jack told you about the tape, right?" I groan to myself. Fuuuuuuuck. Did I confess to something he didn't even know about?

Theo nods somberly.

"OK, what is going on? How are you still...?" Friends if Jack told Theo about the tape?

"You taped me without my consent," Theo says.

I burn with shame. But I nod.

"Uncool," Theo says.

Jack clears his throat loudly. It sounds like he says, "Hypocrite says what?" somewhere underneath. Theo turns to give Jack a look that silences him.

I nod, head bent. He's right. Fucking uncool. I let the money get the better of me.

Theo pushes me, shoves me in the shoulder and I stumble back. I snap my head up, fists curling. I won't fight him, but I will defend myself.

But he's laughing. "Dude, I did the same thing."

"Wh... what?"

"I fucked up and tried to blackmail Jack and... and some other people. I pissed a lot of friends off. And you know how hard it is to make people like me."

I can barely process, standing there like a jerk, fists still lightly clenched. "You're not mad?"

"Shit yeah. You shouldn't have done that."

"Theo, I'm sorry—" The speech I've been practicing since I got in the car.

"Shut up for a minute," he says. I do. He comes closer. "You made me realize what I'd done was... I was an asshole. I meant it as a joke, but I used it to my advantage. And by the time I realized I'd taken it too far, I'd already pissed Jack off so bad he wasn't talking to me."

That flare of jealousy. I tamp it down. I want Theo to have friends. I want him to be happy.

"Jack paid you to make that tape," Theo says.

I nod. No hiding from what I'd done now.

Theo reaches out and punches me playfully on the arm. He smiles. "It kind of saved my friendship."

"What? I'm sorry, what?"

Theo shrugs, all good-natured athleticism, casual. "Yeah. I've got something on Jack, he's got something on me. We're equal again."

"Theo that's not how blackmail—"

"Sure it does."

I look past Theo at Jack. He's checking his phone, face lit up by the screen so I know he's not really paying attention to us. Or he's giving us privacy.

"So we're good?" I ask.

Theo says, "Well, you should apologize."

I laugh, relieved. But then get somber. For everything Theo messes up being socially awkward, I have to admit that there is something utterly honest and real about him. He doesn't play any games— hell, I don't think he would know how.

"I'm sorry I helped blackmail you. That was wrong. I won't do it again."

He nods. "Was it your plan?"

I say, "I knew about it. I hadn't planned on being on the tape—"

Theo grins. "You *are* on the tape though."

I take a deep breath. "Yeah." I hate that I'm going to have to ruin this happy whatever-it-is between us. But I came here to apologize. "It wasn't my intent to out you like that."

Theo leans in, hushed and intimate. "Let me tell you a secret."

His scent, the way he smiles at me, the way I have to crane my neck up to meet his gaze. These strange tingles run through me. The fact that he's this close to me in front of Jack, his best friend, makes me feel even more special.

"What's that?" I barely get the words out.

"I don't mind if people know I got together with you."

I can't breathe. He smiles down at me. Tilts forward, kisses me on the mouth, right there on Jack's lawn, where anyone and everyone might see us.

Which is when I realize I don't mind either.

"I think I'm falling for you," I say out of nowhere when the kiss breaks, and cringe. Usually, I'm cooler than that. Usually, I know myself better than that.

He kisses me back, smiling proudly, like for once I am the awkward dork saying all the wrong things and he is the smooth, confident one.

"Everyone does," Theo crows.

IF YOU LOVED THIS STORY AND WANT MORE, IT'S A SPIN-OFF OF AN ONGOING SERIES CALLED CURIOUS, WHICH FOLLOWS THE MFF ROMANCE OF JACK, HAILEY, AND ELLA. YOU CAN START HERE: HTTPS://WWW.AMAZON.COM/DP/B08HYGLSG1

AND OF COURSE, FIVE-STAR RATINGS AND REVIEWS ARE ALWAYS WELCOME. THEY HELP OTHERS FIND THE STORIES AND ENCOURAGE ME TO KEEP WRITING.

THANKS FOR BEING HERE!

XO,

JESS

ALSO BY JESS SAVAGE

CURIOUS SERIES (MFF Romance)

Curious

Devious

Envious

Flirtatious

Theo Wants (MMF/MM Romance)

GOOD IN THE ZAK SERIES (MFF Romance)

Good in the Zak

Better in the Zak

Chance in the Zak